悅讀莎士比亞經典名劇故事

作者_ Charles and Mary Lamb
譯者 _ Cosmos Language Workshop

羅密歐與茱麗葉
連環錯
無事生非
暴風雨

目錄

Romeo
and Juliet

The Comedy
of Errors

Much Ado About Nothing

The Tempest

中譯

威廉·莎士比亞（William Shakespeare, 1564–1681）

莎士比亞二三事

威廉·莎士比亞（William Shakespeare）出生於英國的史特拉福（Stratford-upon-Avon）。莎士比亞的父親曾任地方議員，母親是地主的女兒。莎士比亞對婦女在廚房或起居室裡勞動的描繪不少，這大概是經由觀察母親所得。他本人也懂得園藝，故作品中的植草種樹表現鮮活。

1571 年，莎士比亞進入公立學校就讀，校內教學多採拉丁文，因此在其作品中到處可見到羅馬詩人奧維德（Ovid）的影子。當時代古典文學的英譯日漸普遍，有學者認為莎士比亞只懂得英語，但這種說法有可議之處。舉例來說，在高登的譯本裡，森林女神只用 Diana 這個名字，而莎士比亞卻在《仲夏夜之夢》一劇中用奧維德原作中的 Titania 一名來稱呼仙后。和莎士比亞有私交的文學家班·強生（Ben Jonson）則曾說，莎翁「懂得一點拉丁文，和一點點希臘文」。

莎士比亞的劇本亦常引用《聖經》典故，在伊麗莎白女王時期，通俗英語中已有很多《聖經》詞語。此外，莎士比亞應該很知悉當時年輕人所流行的遊戲娛樂，當時也應該有巡迴劇團不時前來史特拉福演出。 1575 年，伊麗莎白女王來到郡上時，當地人以化裝遊行、假面戲劇、煙火來款待女王，《仲夏夜之夢》裡就有這種盛會的描繪。

莎士比亞出生地：史特拉福（Stratford-upon-Avon）

環球劇場（Globe Theatre）（1997 年重建）

1582 年，莎士比亞與安・海瑟威（Anne Hathaway）結婚，但這場婚姻顯得草率，連莎士比亞的雙親都因不知情而沒有出席婚禮。 1586 年，他們在倫敦定居下來。 1586 年的倫敦已是英國首都，年輕人莫不想在此大展抱負。史特拉福與倫敦之間的交通頻仍，但對身無長物的人而言，步行仍是最平常的旅行方式。伊麗莎白時期的文學家喜好步行，1618 年，班・強生就曾在倫敦與愛丁堡之間徒步來回。

莎士比亞初抵倫敦的史料不充足，有諸多揣測。其中一說為莎士比亞曾在律師處當職員，因為他在劇本與詩歌中經常提及法律術語。但這種說法站不住腳，因為莎士比亞多有訛用，例如他在《威尼斯商人》和《一報還一報》中提到的法律原理和程序，就有諸多錯誤。事實上，伊麗莎白時期的作家都喜歡引用法律詞彙，這是因為當時的文人和律師時有往來，而且中產階級也常介入訴訟案件，許多法律術語自然為常人所知。莎士比亞樂於援用法律術語，這顯示了他對當代生活和風尚的興趣。莎士比亞自抵達倫敦到告老還鄉，心思始終放在戲劇和詩歌上，不太可能接受法律這門專業領域的訓練。

莎士比亞在倫敦的第一份工作是劇場工作。當時常態營業的劇場有兩個：「劇場」（the Theatre）和「帷幕」（the Curtain）。「劇場」的所有人為詹姆士・波比奇（James Burbage），莎士比亞就在此落腳。「劇場」財務狀況不佳，1596 年波比奇過世，把「劇場」交給兩個兒子，其中一個兒子便是著名的悲劇演員理查・波比奇（Richard Burbage）。後來「劇場」因租約問題無法解決，決定將原有的建築物拆除，在泰晤士河的對面重建，改名為「環球」（the Globe）。不久，「環球」就展開了戲劇史上空前繁榮的時代。

伊麗莎白時期的戲劇表演只有男演員，所有的女性角色都由男性擔任。演員反串時會戴上面具，效果十足，不損故事的意境。莎士比亞本身也是一位出色的演員，曾在《皆大歡喜》和《哈姆雷特》中分別扮演忠僕亞當和國王鬼魂這兩個角色。

莎士比亞很留意演員的說白，這點可從哈姆雷特告誡伶人的對話中窺知一二。莎士比亞熟稔劇場的技術與運作，加上他也是劇場股東，故對劇場的營運和組織都甚有研究。不過，他的志業不在演出或劇場管理，而是劇本和詩歌創作。

1591 年，莎士比亞開始創作戲劇，他師法擅長喜劇的約翰・李利（John Lyly），以及曾寫下轟動一時的悲劇《帖木兒大帝》（*Tamburlaine the Great*）的克里斯多夫・馬婁（Christopher Marlowe）。莎翁戲劇的特色是兼容並蓄，吸收各家長處，而且他也勤奮多產。一直到 1611 年封筆之前，每年平均寫出兩部劇作和三卷詩作。莎士比亞慣於在既有的文學作品中尋找材料，又重視大眾喜好，常能讓平淡無奇的作品廣受喜愛。

在當時，劇本都是賣斷給劇場，不能再賣給出版商，因此莎劇的出版先後，並不能反映其創作的時間先後。莎翁作品的先後順序都由後人所推斷，推測的主要依據是作品題材和韻格。他早期的戲劇作品，無論悲劇或喜劇，性質都很單純。隨著創作的手法逐漸成熟，內容愈來愈複雜深刻，悲喜劇熔冶一爐。

自 1591 年席德尼爵士（Sir Philip Sidney）的十四行詩集發表後，十四行詩（sonnets，另譯為商籟）在英國即普遍受到文人的喜愛與仿傚。其中許多作品承續佩脫拉克（Petrarch）的風格，多描寫愛情的酸甜苦樂。莎士比亞的創作一向很能反應當時的文學風尚，在詩歌體裁鼎盛之時，他也將才華展現在十四行詩上，並將部分作品寫入劇本之中。

莎士比亞的十四行詩主要有兩個主題：婚姻責任和詩歌的不朽。這兩者皆是文藝復興時期詩歌中常見的主題。不少人以為莎士比亞的十四行詩表達了他個人的自省與懺悔，但事實上這些內容有更多是源於他的戲劇天分。

1595 至 1598 年，莎士比亞陸續寫了《羅密歐與茱麗葉》、《仲夏夜之夢》、《馴悍記》、《威尼斯商人》和若干歷史劇，他的詩歌戲劇也在這段時期受到肯定。當時的法蘭西斯 · 梅爾斯（Francis Meres）就將莎士比亞視為最偉大的文學家，他說：「要是繆思會說英語，一定也會喜歡引用莎士比亞的精彩語藻。」「無論是悲劇或喜劇，莎士比亞的表現都是首屈一指。」

闊別故鄉十一年後，莎士比亞於 1596 年返回故居，並在隔年買下名為「新居」（New Place）的房子。那是鎮上第二大的房子，他大幅改建整修，爾後家道日益興盛。莎士比亞大筆的固定收入主要來自表演，而非劇本創作。當時不乏有成功的演員靠演戲發財，甚至有人將這種現象寫成劇本。除了表演，劇場行政和管理的工作，以及宮廷演出的賞賜，都是他的財源。許多文獻均顯示，莎士比亞是個非常關心財富、地產和社會地位的人，讓許多人感到與他的詩人形象有些扞格不入。

伊麗莎白女王過世後，詹姆士一世（James I）於 1603 年登基，他把莎士比亞所屬的劇團納入保護。莎士比亞此時寫了《第十二夜》和佳評如潮的《哈姆雷特》，成就傲視全英格蘭。但他仍謙恭有禮、溫文爾雅，一如十多前年初抵倫敦的樣子，因此也愈發受到大眾的喜愛。

史特拉福聖三一教堂（Holy Trinity Church）
的莎翁紀念雕像和莎翁之墓

從這一年起，莎士比亞開始撰寫悲劇《奧賽羅》。他寫悲劇並非是因為精神壓力或生活變故，而是身為一名劇作家，最終目的就是要寫出優秀的悲劇作品。當時他嘗試以詩入劇，在《哈姆雷特》和《一報還一報》中尤其爐火純青。隨後《李爾王》和《馬克白》問世，一直到四年後的《安東尼與克麗奧佩脫拉》，寫作風格登峰造極。

1609 年，倫敦瘟疫猖獗，隔年，莎士比亞決定告別倫敦，返回史特拉福退隱。1616 年，莎士比亞和老友德雷頓、班・強生聚會時，可能由於喝得過於盡興，回家後發高熱，一病不起。他將遺囑修改完畢後，恰巧在他 52 歲的生日當天去世。

七年後，昔日的劇場友人收錄他的劇本做為全集出版，包括喜劇、歷史劇、悲劇等共 36 部。此書不僅不負莎翁本人所託，也為後人留下珍貴而豐富的文化資源，其中不僅包括美妙動人的詞句，還有各種人物的性格塑造與著墨。

除了作品，莎士比亞本人也在生前受到讚揚。班・強生曾說他是個「正人君子，天性開放自由，想像力出奇，擁有大無畏的思想，言詞溫和，蘊含機智」。也有學者以勇敢、敏感、平衡、幽默和身心健康這五種特質來形容莎士比亞，並說他「將無私的愛奉為至上，認為罪惡的根源是恐懼，而非金錢。」

因為這些劇本刻畫入微，具有知性，有人認為不可能是未受過大學教育的莎士比亞所作，因而引發爭議。有人推測出真正的作者，其中較為人所知的有法蘭西斯・培根（Francis Bacon）和牛津的德維爾公爵（Edward de Vere of Oxford），後者形成了頗具影響力的牛津學派。儘管傳說繪聲繪影，各種假說和研究不斷，但大概沒有人會說莎士比亞是虛構人物。

左：姊姊瑪麗（Mary Lamb, 1764–1847）
右：弟弟查爾斯（Charles Lamb, 1775–1834）

作者簡介：蘭姆姊弟

姊姊瑪麗（Mary Lamb）生於 1764 年，弟弟查爾斯（Charles Lamb）於 1775 年也在倫敦呱呱落地。因為家境不夠寬裕，瑪麗沒有接受過完整的教育。她從小就做針線活，幫忙持家，照顧母親。查爾斯在學生時代結識了詩人柯立芝（Samuel Taylor Coleridge），兩人成為終生的朋友。查爾斯後來因家中經濟困難而輟學，1792 年轉而就職於東印度公司（East India House），這是他謀生的終身職業。

查爾斯在二十歲時一度精神崩潰，瑪麗則因為長年工作過量，在 1796 年突然精神病發，持刀攻擊父母，母親不幸傷重身亡。這件人倫悲劇發生後，瑪麗被判為精神異常，送往精神病院。查爾斯為此放棄自己原本期待的婚姻，以便全心照顧姊姊，使她免於在精神病院終老。

十九世紀的英國教育重視莎翁作品，一般的中產階級家庭也希望孩子早點接觸莎劇。1806 年，文學家兼編輯高德溫（William Godwin）邀請查爾斯協助「少年圖書館」的出版計畫，請他將莎翁的劇本改寫為適合兒童閱讀的故事。

查爾斯接受這項工作後就與瑪麗合作，他負責六齣悲劇，瑪麗負責十四齣喜劇並撰寫前言。瑪麗在後來曾描述説，他們兩人

蘭姆姊弟的《莎士比亞故事集》(*Tales from Shakespeare*)
1922 年版的卷首插畫

「就坐在同一張桌子上改寫，看起來就好像《仲夏夜之夢》裡的荷米雅與海蓮娜一樣。」就這樣，姊弟兩人合力完成了這一系列的莎士比亞故事。《莎士比亞故事集》在 1807 年出版後便大受好評，建立了查爾斯的文學聲譽。

查爾斯的寫作風格獨特，筆法樸實，主題豐富。他將自己的一生，包括童年時代、基督教會學校的生活、東印度公司的光陰、與瑪麗相伴的點點滴滴，以及自己的白日夢、鍾愛的書籍和友人等等，都融入在文章裡，作品充滿細膩情感和豐富的想像力。他的軟弱、怪異、魅力、幽默、口吃，在在都使讀者感到親切熟悉，而獨特的筆法與敘事方式，也使他成為英國出色的散文大師。

1823 年，查爾斯和瑪麗領養了一個孤兒愛瑪。兩年後，查爾斯自東印度公司退休，獲得豐厚的退休金。查爾斯的健康情形和瑪麗的精神狀況卻每況愈下。 1833 年，愛瑪嫁給出版商後，又只剩下姊弟兩人。 1834 年 7 月，由於幼年時代的好友柯立芝去世，查爾斯的精神一蹶不振，沉湎酒精。此年秋天，查爾斯在散步時不慎跌倒，傷及顏面，後來傷口竟惡化至不可收拾的地步，而於年底過世。

查爾斯善與人交，和許多文人都保持良好情誼，又因為他一生對姊姊的照顧不餘遺力，所以也廣受敬佩。查爾斯和瑪麗兩人都終生未婚，查爾斯曾在一篇伊利亞小品中，將他們的狀況形容為「雙重單身」（double singleness）。查爾斯去世後，瑪麗的心理狀態雖然漸趨惡化，但一直到十三年後才辭世。

Romeo and Juliet

羅密歐與茱麗葉

《羅密歐與茱麗葉》導讀

劇情架構

《羅密歐與茱麗葉》是莎士比亞很受歡迎的劇作。根據推測，本劇完成於 1596 年，故事源自十六世紀的義大利小說，敘述祕密戀情受到家庭、命運等限制，或感受到時間的緊迫與壓力而造成不幸結局。莎士比亞創作此劇的主要來源有兩個：

- 布魯克（Arthur Brooke）的《羅密額斯與茱麗葉的悲劇史》（*Tragicall Historye of Romeus and Juliet*）
- 潘特（William Painter）的《羅密歐與茱麗葉塔》（*Rhomeo and Julietta*）

前者尤其提供了故事完整的架構，莎翁的《羅》劇幾乎可說是依據該作品改寫而成。本劇描述維洛那城的兩個望族孟鐵古與柯譜雷，兩家為世仇，但兩家子女羅密歐與茱麗葉卻在一場舞會中墜入情網，並透過修士勞倫斯的證婚，祕密結為夫婦。

完婚當天，兩家人馬在街上鬥毆，柯家的提伯特殺死了羅密歐的好友馬庫修，羅密歐一時激憤，也殺了提伯特。維洛那城的親王於是下令驅逐羅密歐。

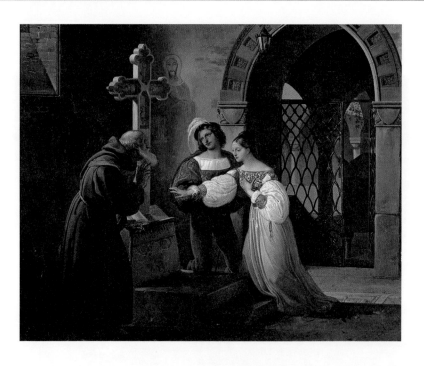

之後，茱麗葉的父親提出一門親事，要她嫁給裴力司伯爵。無助的茱麗葉向勞倫斯修士求助，並接受他的提議喝下一種藥水，以便詐死。修士打算把這個消息告訴羅密歐，叫他到墓穴裡把茱麗葉帶走，但羅密歐始終沒有接到修士的信，只得知茱麗葉死去的消息。他萬分悲痛，當晚趕回維洛那城，服毒殉情。茱麗葉醒來後，看到身旁的羅密歐已經殉情而死，於是就用短劍結束自己的生命。

故事中的愛情簡單而真誠、衝動而自然，故事中的仇恨則是直接而暴力，此種情感和其他的莎劇有顯著不同。本劇的主角都是青少年（羅密歐十八歲，茱麗葉十三歲），情感的方式直接外放，充滿年少情懷。羅密歐在一開場就是個深陷情網、為愛痴狂的年輕人，在遇見茱麗葉之後，又立刻為之瘋狂。他翻越柯家圍牆，遂產生了著名的「樓台景」（the balcony scene）。當他後來知道自己被放逐了以後，整個人癱在地上嚎啕大哭，而茱麗葉對自己情感的表白也同樣直率。

隨著故事的發展，兩人陷入孤立狀況。除了勞倫斯修士，親友都不知道他們的戀情，兩人只能獨自面對苦戀、家庭和逼婚的壓力，還有墓地的恐怖景象。

「命」與「運」

本劇雖然是莎翁早期的悲劇，但從中已經隱約可見莎氏悲劇的雛型：「運」（fortune）與「命」（nature）交織，構成悲劇的因果。例如，勞倫斯修士的信未曾送達羅密歐的手裡，而羅密歐則在衝動的性格下飲鴆自盡。劇中有多處顯示，羅密歐雖有好想法，卻總是缺乏機運，加以行事過於魯莽，終究步入無可挽救的田地。有不少評論家認為茱麗葉顯得較為成熟懂事，她對自己的感情誠實，但不直接違抗父命，對裴力司持適當的禮儀，並有勇氣接受勞倫斯修士的建議，以維護自己的婚姻。

婚姻這一點也反映出清教徒重視神聖婚姻的傳統。英國詩人喬叟（Geoffrey Chaucer, 1345–1400）、史賓賽（Edmund Spenser, 1552/3–1599）或義大利詩人佩托拉克（Petrarch, 1304–1374）的故事，都可見男性追求理想女子的最終目的就是結婚。在伊莉莎白時期，男生合法的結婚年齡為十四歲，女生為十二歲。在望族中，女孩出嫁的年齡會更小，因為父母為確保其地位、財產，會提早為女兒安排婚事，而這也是茱麗葉所面臨的狀況。

本故事最常見的評論是命運與意志的衝突，此劇把兩者放在同等的地位上。對於羅密歐和茱麗葉的悲劇命運，批評家有各種看法。羅勒（John Lawlor）從中古世紀悲劇的標準來看，指出命運並不企圖控制人類，但人類若願意從命運的教訓中學習，則可化解悲劇結果，例如兩大家族最後化解了彼此的仇恨。

愛情的欲望

劇中也有多處呈現觀念的衝突和愛情的矛盾。例如：茱麗葉坦承自己的感情，卻又認為表白過於露骨；勞倫斯修士希望男女主角的結合可以消除兩家的世仇，卻又擔心激情會害了兩人。莎士比亞將這股對愛情的欲望用悲劇作為結束，恰巧顯示了人們對伊莉莎白時期的浪漫主義思想，有著焦慮、悲觀的一面。

人們對欲望的態度會反映出其社會文化，茱麗葉在樓台一景的自我表白，不同於傳統中否定欲望的態度。在當時，女性對愛情的欲望象徵著死亡，但男女主角基於欲望的相許，也為浪漫的個人主義樹立了新觀點。劇中男女主角年紀輕輕就受到愛欲的驅使，私下結婚。這股個人的欲望又和父權產生衝突，因為當時的父親有權為女兒安排婚事。

克里伯（T. J. Cribb）以新柏拉圖的觀念來看本劇的秩序，例如「死亡」代表愛情勝過仇恨，愛與恨這兩種相抗的力量由提伯特這個角色來表現：他反對這對戀人，卻讓他們成為愛情英雄。浪漫時期的作家特別讚揚此劇，例如華茲華斯（William Wordsworth）、柯立芝（Samuel Taylor Coleridge）、雪萊（Percy Bysshe Shelley）、濟慈（John Keats）、蘭姆（Charles Lamb）或韓茲黎（William Hazlitt）。但二十世紀的批評家如卜瑞黎（A. C. Bradley）則傾向於認為，比起莎翁晚期的作品如《李爾王》、《馬克白》等，此劇顯得缺乏力量與深度，不夠成熟。

語言的表現

除了情節和人物之外，本劇的語言也特別受到重視。莎翁在
這個時期偏好人物描寫和詩藝。當時盛行十四行詩，他也
用這種修辭語言來表現戀人的心境。這種寫作方式包括誇飾
（hyperbole）、機智言詞（witty conceit）、似是而非的譎辭
（oxymoron）和反覆（repetition）等等，而其寫作內容則刻意
表現出模糊、暗示和預言，也因此劇中有些對話不像是在刻畫
角色，反倒像是一段詩作。

《羅密歐與茱麗葉》人物表

Romeo	羅密歐	孟家的愛子
Juliet	茱麗葉	柯家的愛女，柯家與孟家是世仇
Benvolio	班夫禮	羅密歐的友人
Mercutio	馬庫修	羅密歐的友人
Tybalt	提伯特	柯家人，茱麗葉的堂兄
Friar Lawrence	勞倫斯修士	主持歐密歐和茱麗葉的婚禮
Paris	裴力司伯爵	父親挑選的女婿，要與茱麗葉結婚

Romeo and Juliet

The two chief families in Verona were the rich Capulets and the Montagues. There had been an old quarrel between these families, which was grown to such a height, and so deadly was the enmity[1] between them, that it extended to the remotest kindred, to the followers and retainers[2] of both sides, insomuch that a servant of the house of Montague could not meet a servant of the house of Capulet, nor a Capulet encounter with a Montague by chance, but fierce words and sometimes bloodshed ensued[3]; and frequent were the brawls[4] from such accidental meetings, which disturbed the happy quiet of Verona's streets.

Old Lord Capulet made a great supper, to which many fair ladies and many noble guests were invited. All the admired beauties of Verona were present, and all comers were made welcome if they were not of the house of Montague.

1 enmity [ˈenmɪti] (n.) 仇恨
2 retainer [rɪˈteɪnər] (n.) 〔舊時用法〕僕人
3 ensue [ɪnˈsuː] (v.) 隨著發生
4 brawl [brɑːl] (n.) 大聲的爭吵

At this feast of Capulets, Rosaline, beloved of Romeo, son to the old Lord Montague, was present; and though it was dangerous for a Montague to be seen in this assembly, yet Benvolio, a friend of Romeo, persuaded the young lord to go to this assembly in the disguise of a mask, that he might see his Rosaline, and seeing her, compare her with some choice beauties of Verona, who (he said) would make him think his swan a crow.

Romeo had small faith in Benvolio's words; nevertheless, for the love of Rosaline, he was persuaded to go. For Romeo was a sincere and passionate lover, and one that lost his sleep for love, and fled society to be alone, thinking on Rosaline, who disdained[5] him, and never requited his love, with the least show of courtesy or affection; and Benvolio wished to cure his friend of this love by showing him diversity of ladies and company.

---

5 disdain [dɪs'deɪn] (v.) 藐視

To this feast of Capulets then young Romeo with Benvolio and their friend Mercutio went masked. Old Capulet bid them welcome, and told them that ladies who had their toes unplagued[6] with corns[7] would dance with them. And the old man was light hearted and merry, and said that he had worn a mask when he was young, and could have told a whispering tale in a fair lady's ear.

And they fell to dancing, and Romeo was suddenly struck with the exceeding beauty of a lady who danced there, who seemed to him to teach the torches to burn bright, and her beauty to show by night like a rich jewel worn by a blackamoor[8]; beauty too rich for use, too dear for earth! like a snowy dove trooping with crows (he said), so richly did her beauty and perfections shine above the ladies her companions.

While he uttered these praises, he was overheard by Tybalt, a nephew of Lord Capulet, who knew him by his voice to be Romeo.

---

6 unplagued [ʌnˈpleɪɡd] (a.) 未受苦的
7 corn [kɔːrn] (n.) 雞眼
8 blackamoor [ˈblækəmɔːr] (n.) 〔輕蔑用法〕黑人

And this Tybalt, being of a fiery[9] and passionate temper, could not endure that a Montague should come under cover of a mask, to fleer[10] and scorn (as he said) at their solemnities. And he stormed and raged exceedingly, and would have struck young Romeo dead.

But his uncle, the old Lord Capulet, would not suffer him to do any injury at that time, both out of respect to his guests, and because Romeo had borne himself like a gentleman, and all tongues in Verona bragged of him to be a virtuous and well-governed youth.

Tybalt, forced to be patient against his will, restrained himself, but swore that this vile Montague should at another time dearly pay for his intrusion.

The dancing being done, Romeo watched the place where the lady stood; and under favor of his masking habit, which might seem to excuse in part the liberty, he presumed[11] in the gentlest manner to take her by the hand, calling it a shrine, which if he profaned[12] by touching it, he was a blushing pilgrim, and would kiss it for atonement[13].

"Good pilgrim," answered the lady, "your devotion shows by far too mannerly and too courtly: saints have hands, which pilgrims may touch, but kiss not."

"Have not saints lips, and pilgrims, too?" said Romeo.

"Ay," said the lady, "lips which they must use in prayer."

---

9 fiery ['faɪri] (a.) 易怒的；暴躁的
10 fleer [flɪr] (v.) 嘲笑
11 presume [prɪ'zuːm] (v.) 擅自（做）；冒昧
12 profane [prə'feɪn] (v.) 褻瀆
13 atonement [ə'toʊnmənt] (n.) 彌補；贖罪

"Oh, then, my dear saint," said Romeo, "hear my prayer, and grant it, lest I despair."

In such like allusions[14] and loving conceits[15] they were engaged, when the lady was called away to her mother. And Romeo inquiring who her mother was, discovered that the lady whose peerless beauty he was so much struck with, was young Juliet, daughter and heir to the Lord Capulet, the great enemy of the Montagues; and that he had unknowingly engaged his heart to his foe.

This troubled him, but it could not dissuade[16] him from loving. As little rest had Juliet, when she found that the gentleman that she had been talking with was Romeo and a Montague, for she had been suddenly smit[17] with the same hasty and inconsiderate passion for Romeo, which he had conceived for her; and a prodigious[18] birth of love it seemed to her, that she must love her enemy, and that her affections should settle there, where family considerations should induce her chiefly to hate.

---

14 allusion [əˈluːʒən] (n.) 暗示；間接提及
15 conceit [kənˈsiːt] (n.) 詼諧機智的思想或語句
16 dissuade [dɪˈsweɪd] (v.) 勸阻
17 smite [smaɪt] (v.)〔古〕痛擊（過去分詞的舊時用法為 smit，現代用法為 smitten/smote）
18 prodigious [prəˈdɪdʒəs] (a.) 奇異的

It being midnight, Romeo with his companions departed; but they soon missed him, for, unable to stay away from the house where he had left his heart, he leaped the wall of an orchard which was at the back of Juliet's house. Here he had not been long, ruminating[19] on his new love, when Juliet appeared above at a window, through which her exceeding beauty seemed to break like the light of the sun in the east; and the moon, which shone in the orchard with a faint light, appeared to Romeo as if sick and pale with grief at the superior luster[20] of this new sun.

And she, leaning her cheek upon her hand, he passionately wished himself a glove upon that hand, that he might touch her cheek. She all this while thinking herself alone, fetched a deep sigh, and exclaimed, "Ah me!"

Romeo, enraptured[21] to bear her speak, said softly, and unheard by her, "Oh, speak again, bright angel, for such you appear, being over my head, like a winged messenger from heaven whom mortals fall back to gaze upon."

19 ruminate ['ruːmɪneɪt] (v.) 反覆思索
20 luster ['lʌstər] (n.) 光澤；光輝
21 enraptured [ɪn'ræptʃərd] (a.) 狂喜的

She, unconscious of being overheard, and full of the new passion which that night's adventure had given birth to, called upon her lover by name (whom she supposed absent): "Oh, Romeo, Romeo!" said she, "wherefore[22] art thou Romeo? Deny thy father, and refuse thy name, for my sake; or if thou wilt not, be but my sworn love, and I no longer will be a Capulet."

Romeo, having this encouragement, would fain have spoken, but he was desirous of hearing more; and the lady continued her passionate discourse with herself (as she thought), still chiding Romeo for being Romeo and a Montague, and wishing him some other name, or that he would put away that hated name, and for that name which was no part of himself, he should take all herself.

At this loving word Romeo could no longer refrain[23], but taking up the dialogue as if her words had been addressed to him personally, and not merely in fancy, he bade her call him Love, or by whatever other name she pleased, for he was no longer Romeo, if that name was displeasing to her.

---

22 wherefore ['werfɔːr] (adv.) 〔舊時用法〕為何
23 refrain [rɪ'freɪn] (v.) 克制

Juliet, alarmed to hear a man's voice in the garden, did not at first know who it was, that by favor of the night and darkness had thus stumbled upon the discovery of her secret; but when he spoke again, though her ears had not yet drunk a hundred words of that tongue's uttering, yet so nice is a lover's hearing, that she immediately knew him to be young Romeo, and she expostulated[24] with him on the danger to which he had exposed himself by climbing the orchard walls, for if any of her kinsmen should find him there, it would be death to him being a Montague.

"Alack!" said Romeo, "there is more peril in your eye, than in twenty of their swords. Do you but look kind upon me, lady, and I am proof against their enmity. Better my life should be ended by their hate, than that hated life should be prolonged, to live without your love."

"How came you into this place," said Juliet, "and by whose direction?"

"Love directed me," answered Romeo. "I am no pilot, yet wert thou as far apart from me, as that vast shore which is washed with the farthest sea, I should venture for such merchandise."

24 expostulate [ɪkˈspɑːstʃuleɪt] (v.) 告誡；勸誡

A crimson[25] blush came over Juliet's face, yet unseen by Romeo by reason of the night, when she reflected upon the discovery which she had made, yet not meaning to make it, of her love to Romeo.

She would fain have recalled her words, but that was impossible; fain would she have stood upon form, and have kept her lover at a distance, as the custom of discreet[26] ladies is, to frown and be perverse[27], and give their suitors harsh denials at first; to stand off, and affect a coyness[28] or indifference, where they most love, that their lovers may not think them too lightly or too easily won; for the difficulty of attainment increases the value of the object.

But there was no room in her case for denials, or puttings off, or any of the customary arts of delay and protracted[29] courtship. Romeo had heard from her own tongue, when she did not dream that he was near her, a confession of her love.

---

25 crimson ['krɪmzən] (a.) 深紅色的
26 discreet [dɪ'skriːt] (a.) 謹慎的
27 perverse [pər'vɜːrs] (a.) 故意作惡的
28 coyness ['kɔɪnɪs] (n.) 害羞；嬌羞忸怩
29 protracted [prə'træktɪd] (a.) 拖延時間的

So with an honest frankness, which the novelty of her situation excused, she confirmed the truth of what he had before heard, and addressing him by the name of *Fair Montague* (love can sweeten a sour name), she begged him not to impute[30] her easy yielding to levity[31] or an unworthy mind, but that he must lay the fault of it (if it were a fault) upon the accident of the night which had so strangely discovered her thoughts.

And she added, that though her behavior to him might not be sufficiently prudent[32], measured by the custom of her sex, yet that she would prove more true than many whose prudence was dissembling[33], and their modesty artificial cunning.

Romeo was beginning to call the heavens to witness, that nothing was farther from his thoughts than to impute a shadow of dishonor to such an honored lady, when she stopped him, begging him not to swear; for although she joyed in him, yet she had no joy of that night's contract: it was too rash, too unadvised, too sudden.

---

30 impute [ɪmˈpjuːt] (v.) 歸於
31 levity [ˈlevɪti] (n.) 輕率
32 prudent [ˈpruːdənt] (a.) 審慎小心的
33 dissemble [dɪˈsembəl] (v.) 掩飾

But he being urgent with her to exchange a vow of love with him that night, she said that she already had given him hers before he requested it; meaning, when he overheard her confession; but she would retract what she then bestowed[34], for the pleasure of giving it again, for her bounty[35] was as infinite as the sea, and her love as deep.

From this loving conference she was called away by her nurse, who slept with her, and thought it time for her to be in bed, for it was near to daybreak; but hastily returning, she said three or four words more to Romeo, the purport[36] of which was, that if his love was indeed honorable, and his purpose marriage, she would send a messenger to him tomorrow, to appoint a time for their marriage, when she would lay all her fortunes at his feet, and follow him as her lord through the world.

While they were settling this point, Juliet was repeatedly called for by her nurse, and went in and returned, and went and returned again, for she seemed as jealous of Romeo going from her, as a young girl of her bird, which she will let hop a little from her hand, and pluck it back with a silken thread; and Romeo was as loath[37] to part as she; for the sweetest music to lovers is the sound of each other's tongues at night.

34 bestow [bɪˈstoʊ] (v.) 賜與
35 bounty [ˈbaʊnti] (n.) 慷慨
36 purport [pɜːrˈpɔːrt] (n.) 主旨
37 loath [loʊθ] (a.) 不願意做某事

But at last they parted, wishing mutually sweet sleep and rest for that night. The day was breaking when they parted, and Romeo, who was too full of thoughts of his mistress and that blessed meeting to allow him to sleep, instead of going home, bent his course to a monastery[38] hard by, to find Friar[39] Lawrence.

The good friar was already up at his devotions, but seeing young Romeo abroad so early, he conjectured[40] rightly that he had not been abed that night, but that some distemper[41] of youthful affection had kept him waking.

He was right in imputing the cause of Romeo's wakeful-ness to love, but he made a wrong guess at the object, for he thought that his love for Rosaline had kept him waking.

But when Romeo revealed his new passion for Juliet, and requested the assistance of the friar to marry them that day, the holy man lifted up his eyes and hands in a sort of wonder at the sudden change in Romeo's affections, for he had been privy[42] to all Romeo's love for Rosaline, and his many complaints of her disdain; and he said, that young men's love lay not truly in their hearts, but in their eyes.

38 monastery [ˈmɑːnəsteri] (n.) 修道院

39 friar [ˈfraɪər] (n.) 修道士

40 conjecture [kənˈdʒektʃər] (v.) 猜想；推測

41 distemper [dɪˈstempər] (n.) 思緒混亂

42 privy [ˈprɪvi] (a.) 知情的

But Romeo replying, that he himself had often chidden[43] him for doting on Rosaline, who could not love him again, whereas Juliet both loved and was beloved by him, the friar assented in some measure to his reasons; and thinking that a matrimonial[44] alliance between young Juliet and Romeo might happily be the means of making up the long breach between the Capulets and the Montagues; which no one more lamented[45] than this good friar, who was a friend to both the families and had often interposed[46] his mediation to make up the quarrel without effect; partly moved by policy, and partly by his fondness for young Romeo, to whom he could deny nothing, the old man consented to join their hands in marriage.

Now was Romeo blessed indeed, and Juliet, who knew his intent from a messenger which she had despatched[47] according to promise, did not fail to be early at the cell of Friar Lawrence, where their hands were joined in holy marriage; the good friar praying the heavens to smile upon that act, and in the union of this young Montague and young Capulet to bury the old strife and long dissensions[48] of their families.

43 chide [tʃaɪd] (v.) 責罵

44 matrimonial [ˌmætrɪ'mouniəl] (a.) 婚姻的

45 lament [lə'ment] (v.) 悲傷；惋惜

46 interpose [ˌɪntər'pouz] (v.) 調停

47 despatch [dɪ'spætʃ] (v.) 派遣

48 dissension [dɪ'senʃən] (n.) 紛爭

49 impetuous [ɪmˈpetʃuəs] (a.) 衝動魯莽的

50 moderate [ˈmɑːdəreɪt] (v.) 緩和；減輕

51 appellation [ˌæpəˈleɪʃən] (n.) 名稱；稱呼

52 villain [ˈvɪlən] (n.) 惡徒

The ceremony being over, Juliet hastened home, where she stayed impatient for the coming of night, at which time Romeo promised to come and meet her in the orchard, where they had met the night before; and the time between seemed as tedious to her, as the night before some great festival seems to an impatient child, that has got new finery which it may not put on till the morning.

That same day, about noon, Romeo's friends, Benvolio and Mercutio, walking through the streets of Verona, were met by a party of the Capulets with the impetuous[49] Tybalt at their head. This was the same angry Tybalt who would have fought with Romeo at old Lord Capulet's feast.

He, seeing Mercutio, accused him bluntly of associating with Romeo, a Montague. Mercutio, who had as much fire and youthful blood in him as Tybalt, replied to this accusation with some sharpness; and in spite of all Benvolio could say to moderate[50] their wrath, a quarrel was beginning, when Romeo himself passing that way, the fierce Tybalt turned from Mercutio to Romeo, and gave him the disgraceful appellation[51] of villain[52].

Romeo wished to avoid a quarrel with Tybalt above all men, because he was the kinsman of Juliet, and much beloved by her; besides, this young Montague had never thoroughly entered into the family quarrel, being by nature wise and gentle, and the name of a Capulet, which was his dear lady's name, was now rather a charm to allay[53] resentment[54], than a watchword to excite fury.

So he tried to reason with Tybalt, whom he saluted mildly by the name of *Good Capulet*, as if he, though Montague, had some secret pleasure in uttering that name; but Tybalt, who hated all Montagues as he hated hell, would hear no reason, but drew his weapon; and Mercutio, who knew not of Romeo's secret motive for desiring peace with Tybalt, but looked upon his present forbearance as a sort of calm dishonorable submission[55], with many disdainful words provoked[56] Tybalt to the prosecution[57] of his first quarrel with him; and Tybalt and Mercutio fought, till Mercutio fell, receiving his death's wound while Romeo and Benvolio were vainly endeavoring to part the combatants[58].

53 allay [əˈleɪ] (v.) 減輕；緩和

54 resentment [rɪˈzentmənt] (n.) 憤恨

55 submission [səbˈmɪʃən] (n.) 服從；忠順

56 provoke [prəˈvouk] (v.) 迫使

57 prosecution [ˌprɑːsɪˈkjuːʃən] (n.) 進行；繼續從事

58 combatant [kəmˈbætənt] (n.) 戰鬥人員

Mercutio being dead, Romeo kept his temper no longer, but returned the scornful appellation of villain which Tybalt had given him; and they fought till Tybalt was slain[59] by Romeo.

This deadly broil falling out in the midst of Verona at noonday, the news of it quickly brought a crowd of citizens to the spot, and among them the old Lords Capulet and Montague, with their wives; and soon after arrived the prince himself, who being related to Mercutio, whom Tybalt had slain, and having had the peace of his government often disturbed by these brawls of Montagues and Capulets, came determined to put the law in strictest force against those who should be found to be offenders.

Benvolio, who had been eye witness to the fray[60], was commanded by the prince to relate the origin of it, which he did, keeping as near the truth as he could without injury to Romeo, softening and excusing the part which his friends took in it.

Lady Capulet, whose extreme grief for the loss of her kinsman Tybalt made her keep no bounds in her revenge, exhorted[61] the prince to do strict justice upon his murderer, and to pay no attention to Benvolio's representation, who, being Romeo's friend and a Montague, spoke partially. Thus she pleaded[62] against her new son-in-law, but she knew not yet that he was her son-in-law and Juliet's husband.

---

59 slay [sleɪ] (v.) 殺死（動詞變化：slew; slain; slaying）
60 fray [freɪ] (n.) 打鬥；爭吵
61 exhort [ɪgˈzɔːrt] (v.) 力勸
62 plead [pliːd] (v.) 抗辯

On the other hand was to be seen Lady Montague pleading for her child's life, and arguing with some justice that Romeo had done nothing worthy of punishment in taking the life of Tybalt, which was already forfeited to the law by his having slain Mercutio.

The prince, unmoved by the passionate exclamations of these women, on a careful examination of the facts, pronounced his sentence, and by that sentence Romeo was banished [63] from Verona.

Heavy news to young Juliet, who had been but a few hours a bride, and now by this decree [64] seemed everlastingly divorced! When the tidings reached her, she at first gave way to rage against Romeo, who had slain her dear cousin.

She called him a beautiful tyrant, a fiend [65] angelical, a ravenous dove, a lamb with a wolf's nature, a serpent-heart hid with a flowering face, and other like contradictory names, which denoted [66] the struggles in her mind between her love and her resentment.

---

63 banish ['bænɪʃ] (v.) 放逐；驅逐出境
64 decree [dɪ'kriː] (n.) 法令；政令
65 fiend [fiːnd] (n.) 窮凶惡極的人
66 denote [dɪ'nout] (v.) 指出；指示

But in the end love got the mastery, and the tears which she shed for grief that Romeo had slain her cousin, turned to drops of joy that her husband lived whom Tybalt would have slain. Then came fresh tears, and they were altogether of grief for Romeo's banishment. That word was more terrible to her than the death of many Tybalts.

Romeo, after the fray, had taken refuge in Friar Lawrence's cell, where he was first made acquainted with the prince's sentence, which seemed to him far more terrible than death. To him it appeared there was no world out of Verona's walls, no living out of the sight of Juliet. Heaven was there where Juliet lived, and all beyond was purgatory[67], torture, hell.

The good friar would have applied the consolation of philosophy to his griefs; but this frantic[68] young man would hear of none, but like a madman he tore his hair and threw himself all along upon the ground, as he said, to take the measure of his grave. From this unseemly state he was roused by a message from his dear lady, which a little revived him; and then the friar took the advantage to expostulate with him on the unmanly weakness which he had shown.

He had slain Tybalt, but would he also slay himself, slay his dear lady, who lived but in his life? The noble form of man, he said, was but a shape of wax when it wanted the courage which should keep it firm. The law had been lenient[69] to him, that instead of death, which he had incurred[70], had pronounced by the prince's mouth only banishment. He had slain Tybalt, but Tybalt would have slain him: there was a sort of happiness in that. Juliet was alive, and (beyond all hope) had become his dear wife; therein he was most happy.

All these blessings, as the friar made them out to be, did Romeo put from him like a sullen[71] misbehaved wench[72]. And the friar bade him beware, for such as despaired (he said) died miserable.

67 purgatory ['pɜːrgətɔːri] (n.) 煉獄
68 frantic ['fræntɪk] (a.) 狂亂的
69 lenient ['liːniənt] (a.) 寬大的；仁慈的
70 incur [ɪn'kɜːr] (v.) 招致；蒙受
71 sullen ['sʌlən] (a.) 繃著臉的；慍怒的
72 wench [wentʃ] (n.) 少女；少婦

Then when Romeo was a little calmed, he counseled him that he should go that night and secretly take his leave of Juliet, and thence[73] proceed straightways to Mantua, at which place he should sojourn[74], till the friar found fit occasion to publish his marriage, which might be a joyful means of reconciling[75] their families; and then he did not doubt but the prince would be moved to pardon him, and he would return with twenty times more joy than he went forth with grief.

Romeo was convinced by these wise counsels of the friar, and took his leave to go and seek his lady, proposing to stay with her that night, and by daybreak pursue his journey alone to Mantua; to which place the good friar promised to send him letters from time to time, acquainting him with the state of affairs at home.

That night Romeo passed with his dear wife, gaining secret admission to her chamber, from the orchard in which he had heard her confession of love the night before. That had been a night of unmixed joy and rapture; but the pleasures of this night, and the delight which these lovers took in each other's society, were sadly allayed with the prospect of parting, and the fatal adventures of the past day.

73 thence [ðens] (adv.) 由彼處
74 sojourn ['soʊdʒɜːrn] (v.) 逗留；寄居
75 reconcile ['rekənsaɪl] (v.) 和解

The unwelcome daybreak seemed to come too soon, and when Juliet heard the morning song of the lark, she would have persuaded herself that it was the nightingale, which sings by night; but it was too truly the lark which sang, and a discordant[76] and unpleasing note it seemed to her, and the streaks[77] of day in the east too certainly pointed out that it was time for these lovers to part.

Romeo took his leave of his dear wife with a heavy heart, promising to write to her from Mantua every hour in the day; and when he had descended from her chamber-window, as he stood below her on the ground, in that sad foreboding state of mind in which she was, he appeared to her eyes as one dead in the bottom of a tomb. Romeo's mind misgave[78] him in like manner. But now he was forced hastily to depart, for it was death for him to be found within the walls of Verona after daybreak.

76 discordant [dɪs'kɔːrdənt] (a.) 不和諧的
77 streak [striːk] (n.) 光線
78 misgive [mɪs'gɪv] (v.) 使擔心；使不安

This was but the beginning of the tragedy of this pair of star-crossed lovers. Romeo had not been gone many days before the old Lord Capulet proposed a match for Juliet. The husband he had chosen for her, not dreaming that she was married already, was Count Paris, a gallant[79], young, and noble gentleman, no unworthy suitor to the young Juliet, if she had never seen Romeo.

The terrified Juliet was in a sad perplexity[80] at her father's offer. She pleaded her youth unsuitable to marriage, the recent death of Tybalt, which had left her spirits too weak to meet a husband with any face of joy, and how indecorous[81] it would show for the family of the Capulets to be celebrating a nuptial[82] feast, when his funeral solemnities were hardly over. She pleaded every reason against the match, but the true one, namely, that she was married already.

But Lord Capulet was deaf to all her excuses, and in a peremptory[83] manner ordered her to get ready, for by the following Thursday she should be married to Paris. And having found her a husband, rich, young and noble, such as the proudest maid in Verona might joyfully accept, he could not bear that out of an affected coyness, as he construed[84] her denial, she should oppose obstacles to her own good fortune.

79 gallant [ˈgælənt] (a.) 英勇的
80 perplexity [pərˈplɛksɪti] (n.) 困惑
81 indecorous [ɪnˈdɛkərəs] (a.) 不合禮節的
82 nuptial [ˈnʌpʃəl] (a.) 婚禮的；結婚的 (n.) 結婚；婚禮
83 peremptory [pəˈrɛmptəri] (a.) 專橫的；獨斷的
84 construe [kənˈstruː] (v.) 解釋；理解為

In this extremity Juliet applied to the friendly friar, always her counselor in distress, and he asking her if she had resolution to undertake a desperate remedy, and she answering that she would go into the grave alive rather than marry Paris, her own dear husband living; he directed her to go home, and appear merry, and give her consent to marry Paris, according to her father's desire, and on the next night, which was the night before the marriage, to drink off the contents of a phial[85] which he then gave her, the effect of which would be that for two-and-forty hours after drinking it she should appear cold and lifeless; and when the bridegroom came to fetch her in the morning, he would find her to appearance dead; that then she would be borne, as the manner in that country was, uncovered on a bier[86], to be buried in the family vault[87]; that if she could put off womanish fear, and consent to this terrible trial, in forty-two hours after swallowing the liquid (such was its certain operation) she would be sure to awake, as from a dream; and before she should awake, he would let her husband know their drift, and he should come in the night, and bear her thence to Mantua.

85 phial [ˈfaɪəl] (n.) 小瓶藥水
86 bier [bɪr] (n.) 棺架；屍架
87 vault [vɑːlt] (n.) 墓穴

Love, and the dread of marrying Paris, gave young Juliet strength to undertake this horrible adventure; and she took the phial of the friar, promising to observe his directions.

Going from the monastery, she met the young Count Paris, and, modestly dissembling, promised to become his bride. This was joyful news to the Lord Capulet and his wife. It seemed to put youth into the old man; and Juliet, who had displeased him exceedingly, by her refusal of the count, was his darling again, now she promised to be obedient.

All things in the house were in a bustle[88] against the approaching nuptials. No cost was spared to prepare such festival rejoicings as Verona had never before witnessed.

On the Wednesday night Juliet drank off the potion. She had many misgivings lest the friar, to avoid the blame which might be imputed to him for marrying her to Romeo, had given her poison; but then he was always known for a holy man.

---

88 bustle ['bʌsəl] (n.) 慌忙

Then lest she should awake before the time that Romeo was to come for her; whether the terror of the place, a vault full of dead Capulets' bones, and where Tybalt, all bloody, lay festering[89] in his shroud[90], would not be enough to drive her distracted. Again she thought of all the stories she had heard of spirits haunting the places where their bodies were bestowed. But then her love for Romeo, and her aversion[91] for Paris returned, and she desperately swallowed the draught[92], and became insensible.

When young Paris came early in the morning with music to awaken his bride, instead of a living Juliet, her chamber presented the dreary spectacle of a lifeless corse[93].

What death to his hopes! What confusion then reigned through the whole house! Poor Paris lamenting his bride, whom most detestable[94] death had beguiled[95] him of, had divorced from him even before their hands were joined.

89 fester ['fɛstər] (v.) 傷口化膿潰爛

90 shroud [ʃraʊd] (n.) 壽衣

91 aversion [ə'vɜːrʒən] (n.) 嫌惡

92 draught [dræft] (n.) 一飲（之量）

93 corse [kɔːrs] (n.)〔詩的用法〕屍體

94 detestable [dɪ'tɛstəbəl] (a.) 可恨的

95 beguile [bɪ'gaɪl] (v.) 欺騙

25

But still more piteous it was to hear the mournings of the old Lord and Lady Capulet, who having but this one, one poor loving child to rejoice and solace[96] in, cruel death had snatched[97] her from their sight, just as these careful parents were on the point of seeing her advanced (as they thought) by a promising and advantageous match.

Now all things that were ordained[98] for the festival were turned from their properties to do the office of a black funeral. The wedding cheer served for a sad burial feast, the bridal hymns were changed for sullen dirges[99], the sprightly instruments to melancholy bells, and the flowers that should have been strewed[100] in the bride's path, now served but to strew her corse. Now, instead of a priest to marry her, a priest was needed to bury her; and she was borne to church indeed, not to augment[101] the cheerful hopes of the living, but to swell[102] the dreary numbers of the dead.

96 solace ['sɑːlɪs] (v.) 安慰
97 snatch [snætʃ] (v.) 攫取
98 ordain [ɔːr'deɪn] (v.) 注定
99 dirge [dɜːrdʒ] (n.) 輓歌
100 strew [struː] (v.) 撒……於表面上
101 augment ['ɔːɡˌment] (v.) 增加；增大
102 swell [swel] (v.) 使增大、增厚或加強

Bad news, which always travels faster than good, now brought the dismal[103] story of his Juliet's death to Romeo, at Mantua, before the messenger could arrive, who was sent from Friar Lawrence to apprise[104] him that these were mock funerals only, and but the shadow and representation of death, and that his dear lady lay in the tomb but for a short while, expecting when Romeo would come to release her from that dreary mansion.

Just before, Romeo had been unusually joyful and light-hearted. He had dreamed in the night that he was dead (a strange dream, that gave a dead man leave to think), and that his lady came and found him dead, and breathed such life with kisses in his lips, that he revived, and was an emperor!

---

103 dismal ['dɪzməl] (a.) 陰沉的
104 apprise [ə'praɪz] (v.) 通知

26

And now that a messenger came from Verona, he thought surely it was to confirm some good news which his dreams had presaged[105]. But when the contrary to this flattering vision appeared, and that it was his lady who was dead in truth, whom he could not revive by any kisses, he ordered horses to be got ready, for he determined that night to visit Verona, and to see his lady in her tomb.

And as mischief is swift to enter into the thoughts of desperate men, he called to mind a poor apothecary[106], whose shop in Mantua he had lately passed, and from the beggarly appearance of the man, who seemed famished, and the wretched show in his show of empty boxes ranged on dirty shelves, and other tokens[107] of extreme wretchedness, he had said at the time (perhaps having some misgivings that his own disastrous life might haply meet with a conclusion so desperate):

"If a man were to need poison, which by the law of Mantua it is death to sell, here lives a poor wretch who would sell it him."

---

105 presage ['prɛsɪdʒ] (v.) 預言
106 apothecary [ə'pɑːθɪkeri] (n.) 藥劑師；藥材商
107 token ['toukən] (n.) 象徵

27

These words of his now came into his mind, and he sought out the apothecary, who after some pretended scruples[108], Romeo offering him gold, which his poverty could not resist, sold him a poison, which, if he swallowed, he told him, if he had the strength of twenty men, would quickly despatch him.

With this poison he set out for Verona, to have a sight of his dear lady in her tomb, meaning, when he had satisfied his sight, to swallow the poison, and be buried by her side.

He reached Verona at midnight, and found the church-yard, in the midst of which was situated the ancient tomb of the Capulets. He had provided a light, and a spade, and wrenching iron, and was proceeding to break open the monument, when he was interrupted by a voice, which by the name of *vile Montague*, bade him desist[109] from his unlawful business.

---

108 scruple ['skruːpəl] (n.) 良心不安
109 desist [dɪ'sɪst] (v.) 停止

It was the young Count Paris, who had come to the tomb of Juliet at that unseasonable time of night, to strew flowers and to weep over the grave of her that should have been his bride. He knew not what an interest Romeo had in the dead, but knowing him to be a Montague, and (as he supposed) a sworn foe to all the Capulets, he judged that he was come by night to do some villainous shame to the dead bodies; therefore in an angry tone he bade him desist; and as a criminal, condemned by the laws of Verona to die if he were found within the walls of the city, he would have apprehended[110] him.

Romeo urged Paris to leave him, and warned him by the fate of Tybalt, who lay buried there, not to provoke his anger, or draw down another sin upon his head by forcing him to kill him.

But the count in scorn refused his warning, and laid hands on him as a felon[111], which Romeo resisting, they fought, and Paris fell.

---

110 apprehend [ˌæprɪˈhend] (v.) 逮捕
111 felon [ˈfelən] (n.) 重罪犯

28

When Romeo, by the help of a light, came to see who it was that he had slain, that it was Paris, who (he learned in his way from Mantua) should have married Juliet, he took the dead youth by the hand, as one whom misfortune had made a companion, and said that he would bury him in a triumphal grave, meaning in Juliet's grave, which he now opened.

And there lay his lady, as one whom death had no power upon to change a feature or complexion, in her matchless beauty; or as if Death were amorous[112], and the lean abhorred monster kept her there for his delight; for she lay yet fresh and blooming, as she had fallen to sleep when she swallowed that benumbing[113] potion; and near her lay Tybalt in his bloody shroud, whom Romeo seeing, begged pardon of his lifeless corse, and for Juliet's sake called him *cousin*, and said that he was about to do him a favor by putting his enemy to death.

---

112 amorous ['æmərəs] (a.) 多情的
113 benumbing [bɪ'nʌmɪŋ] (a.) 使麻木的

Here Romeo took his last leave of his lady's lips, kissing them; and here he shook the burden of his cross stars from his weary body, swallowing that poison which the apothecary had sold him, whose operation was fatal and real, not like that dissembling potion which Juliet had swallowed, the effect of which was now nearly expiring, and she about to awake to complain that Romeo had not kept his time, or that he had come too soon.

29

For now the hour was arrived at which the friar had promised that she should awake; and he, having learned that his letters which he had sent to Mantua, by some unlucky detention[114] of the messenger, had never reached Romeo, came himself, provided with a pickax[115] and lantern, to deliver the lady from her confinement[116]; but he was surprised to find a light already burning in the Capulets' monument, and to see swords and blood near it, and Romeo and Paris lying breathless by the monument.

Before he could entertain a conjecture, to imagine how these fatal accidents had fallen out, Juliet awoke out of her trance[117], and seeing the friar near her, she remembered the place where she was, and the occasion of her being there, and asked for Romeo, but the friar, hearing a noise, bade her come out of that place of death, and of unnatural sleep, for a greater power than they could contradict had thwarted[118] their intents; and being frightened by the noise of people coming, he fled.

114 detention [dɪ'tenʃən] (n.) 阻止；延遲

115 pickax ['pɪkæks] (n.) 鶴嘴鋤；尖鋤

116 confinement [kən'faɪnmənt] (n.) 限制；監禁

117 trance [træns] (n.) 昏睡狀態

118 thwart [θwɔːrt] (v.) 反對；妨礙

But when Juliet saw the cup closed in her true love's hands, she guessed that poison had been the cause of his end, and she would have swallowed the dregs[119] if any had been left, and she kissed his still warm lips to try if any poison yet did hang upon them; then hearing a nearer noise of people coming, she quickly unsheathed a dagger which she wore, and stabbing herself, died by her true Romeo's side.

The watch by this time had come up to the place. A page belonging to Count Paris, who had witnessed the fight between his master and Romeo, had given the alarm, which had spread among the citizens, who went up and down the streets of Verona confusedly exclaiming, "A Paris! a Romeo! a Juliet!" as the rumor had imperfectly reached them, till the uproar brought Lord Montague and Lord Capulet out of their beds, with the prince, to inquire into the causes of the disturbance.

The friar had been apprehended by some of the watch, coming from the churchyard, trembling, sighing, and weeping, in a suspicious manner. A great multitude being assembled at the Capulets' monument, the friar was demanded by the prince to deliver what he knew of these strange and disastrous accidents.

119 dregs [dregz] (n.) 〔作複數形〕渣滓

And there, in the presence of the old Lords Montague and Capulet, he faithfully related the story of their children's fatal love, the part he took in promoting their marriage, in the hope in that union to end the long quarrels between their families: how Romeo, there dead, was husband to Juliet; and Juliet, there dead, was Romeo's faithful wife; how before he could find a fit opportunity to divulge[120] their marriage, another match was projected for Juliet, who, to avoid the crime of a second marriage, swallowed the sleeping draught (as he advised), and all thought her dead; how meantime he wrote to Romeo, to come and take her thence when the force of the potion should cease, and by what unfortunate miscarriage of the messenger the letters never reached Romeo.

Further than this the friar could not follow the story, nor knew more than that coming himself, to deliver Juliet from that place of death, he found the Count Paris and Romeo slain.

120 divulge [daɪ'vʌldʒ] (v.) 洩露;暴露
121 transaction [træn'zækʃən] (n.) 處置

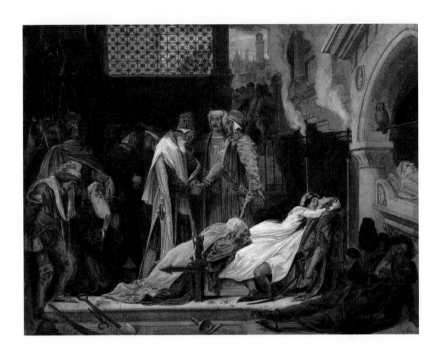

The remainder of the transactions[121] was supplied by the narration of the page who had seen Paris and Romeo fight, and by the servant who came with Romeo from Verona to whom this faithful lover had given letters to be delivered to his father in the event of his death, which made good the friar's words, confessing his marriage with Juliet, imploring the forgiveness of his parents, acknowledging the buying of the poison of the poor apothecary, and his intent in coming to the monument, to die, and lie with Juliet.

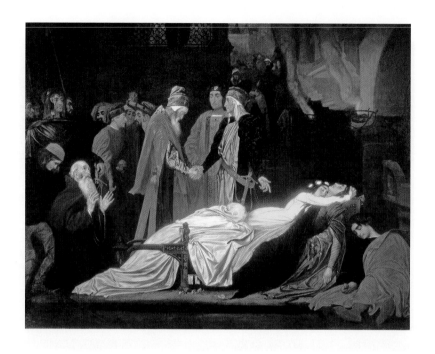

All these circumstances agreed together to clear the friar from any hand he could be supposed to have in these complicated slaughters[122], further than as the unintended consequences of his own well-meant, yet too artificial and subtle contrivances[123].

And the prince, turning to these old lords, Montague and Capulet, rebuked[124] them for their brutal and irrational enmities, and showed them what a scourge[125] heaven had laid upon such offenses, that it had found means even through the love of their children to punish their unnatural hate.

And these old rivals, no longer enemies, agreed to bury their long strife in their children's graves; and Lord Capulet requested Lord Montague to give him his hand, calling him by the name of brother, as if in acknowledgment of the union of their families, by the marriage of the young Capulet and Montague; and saying that Lord Montague's hand (in token of reconcilement) was all he demanded for his daughter's jointure[126]. But Lord Montague said he would give him more, for he would raise her a statue of pure gold, that while Verona kept its name, no figure should be so esteemed for its richness and workmanship as that of the true and faithful Juliet. And Lord Capulet in return said that he would raise another statue to Romeo.

So did these poor old lords, when it was too late, strive to outgo each other in mutual courtesies; while so deadly had been their rage and enmity in past times that nothing but the fearful overthrow of their children (poor sacrifices to their quarrels and dissensions) could remove the rooted hates and jealousies of the noble families.

---

122 slaughter ['slɔːtər] (n.) 殺戮
123 contrivance [kən'traɪvəns] (n.) 想出的辦法
124 rebuke [rɪ'bjuːk] (v.) 指責；非難
125 scourge [skɜːrdʒ] (n.) 懲罰的工具
126 jointure ['dʒɔɪntʃər] (n.) 寡婦所得財產

《羅密歐與茱麗葉》名句選

Chorus　　Two households, both alike in dignity,
　　　　　In fair Verona, where we lay our scene,
　　　　　From ancient grudge break to new mutiny,
　　　　　Where civil blood makes civil hands unclean.
　　　　　From forth the fatal loins of these two foes
　　　　　A pair of star-cross'd lovers take their life;
　　　　　Whose misadventur'd piteous overthrows
　　　　　Doth with their death bury their parents' strife.
　　　　　(Prologue, 1-8)

合唱　　　事發名城維洛那，
　　　　　榮顯相當兩家族，
　　　　　舊日嫌隙起新亂，
　　　　　鮮血沾汙城民手。
　　　　　命運注定兩仇敵，
　　　　　生下可憐之戀人，
　　　　　悽慘不幸之死亡，
　　　　　和解交惡之雙親。

　　　　　（開場詩，1-8 行）

Capulet　 Nay, sit, nay, sit, good cousin Capulet,
　　　　　For you and I are past our dancing days:
　　　　　How long is't now, since last yourself and I
　　　　　Were in a mask?
　　　　　(I, v, 30-33)

柯譜雷　　　啊，坐，啊，坐，好親戚，

　　　　　　你和我都已經跳不起來了：

　　　　　　還記得我們上一次戴面具跳舞是多久以前的事呢？

　　　　　　（第一幕，第五景，30-33 行）

Romeo　　But, soft! what light through yonder window breaks?

　　　　　　It is the east, and Juliet is the sun!—

　　　　　　Arise fair sun, and kill the envious moon,

　　　　　　Who is already sick and pale with grief,

　　　　　　That thou, her maid, art far more fair than she.

　　　　　　(II, ii, 2-6)

羅密歐　　小聲點！窗戶那邊透出的是什麼光？

　　　　　　那就是東方，茱麗葉就是太陽！

　　　　　　升起吧，美麗的太陽，趕走妒忌的月，

　　　　　　她已經傷心得面色慘白，

　　　　　　因為妳是她的侍女，卻比她美多了。

　　　　　　（第二幕，第二景，2-6 行）

Juliet　　　O Romeo, Romeo, wherefore art thou Romeo?

　　　　　　Deny thy father and refuse thy name;

　　　　　　Or, if thou wilt not, be but sworn my love,

　　　　　　And I'll no longer be a Capulet. (II, ii, 33-36)

茱麗葉　　喔，羅密歐，羅密歐，為什麼你偏偏是羅密歐？

　　　　　　不要認你的父親，放棄你的姓氏吧；

　　　　　　你若不願意，就宣誓愛我吧，

　　　　　　那樣我便不再當柯家人。

　　　　　　（第二幕，第二景，33-36 行）

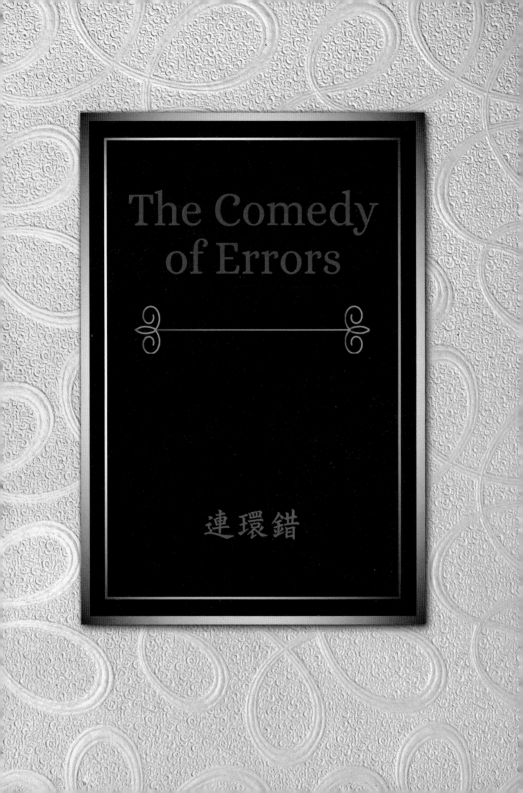

The Comedy of Errors

連環錯

《連環錯》導讀

故事架構與來源

《連環錯》約於 1593–94 年間完成,是莎劇中最短的一部。因為完成的年代最早,所以風格與架構最接近古典喜劇。這齣早期的喜劇,並為後來主題相似但技巧更為成熟的《第十二夜》奠定了基礎。《連環錯》這整個故事都發生在同一天,發生的地點也在同一個地方,主要的情節則在身分錯認一事上,合乎古典戲劇理論中的「三一律」。莎劇少見合乎三一律的架構,除本劇之外,亦見於《暴風雨》。

《連環錯》應是根據羅馬喜劇作家普勞特斯(Plautus, 254–184 B.C.)一齣典型孿生喜劇《孿生兄弟》(*Menaechmi*)的故事大綱改編而成,華納(William Warner)以生動鮮活筆觸將其譯為英文,於 1595 年出版。部分學者認為《連環錯》之所以早一步問世,應該是由於莎士比亞看過拉丁原文或英譯本的初稿。

《孿生兄弟》描述一對雙胞胎兄弟在嬰兒時期分離,長大後在一個城鎮出現。這對孿生兄弟不時遭到誤認,不但令別人惱怒,兩個當事人也感到離奇困惑,一直到劇終兩人相見相認後才水落石出。《連環錯》與《孿生兄弟》的相同之處在於:這些接踵而來的誤會都是由一連串的巧合機運所造成,並非人為的詭計或玩笑。但是莎士比亞除了師法普勞特斯沿用原有的架構之外，又更勝一籌，加入一對孿生奴僕，並且取了相同的名字，使得原本就複雜的誤會，更加糾結難解。

他還借用普勞特斯另一個劇本《安菲特律翁》（ *Amphitruo* ）中的情節：雅卓安娜將丈夫關在門外，與她認定的丈夫在家裡用餐。父親葉吉這個角色也不是莎士比亞所原創的，而是取材於十四世紀的詩人高爾（John Gower）所寫的《泰爾的阿波羅尼斯》（ *Apollonius of Tyre* ）。

孿生兄弟重逢的地點，由掖披丹改為以巫術著稱的以弗所（Ephesus），為小安提弗將誤會解釋為巫術的聯想，提供了絕佳的背景和笑點。此外，葉吉得以在劇終擺脫死刑的威脅，最後闔家團圓，與《孿生兄弟》嘲諷式的賣妻結局大相逕庭，這也是莎士比亞的主意。

「笑劇」

儘管本劇是莎劇劇名中唯一帶有喜劇（comedy）一詞的戲，但長久以來，許多評論家卻堅持這是齣笑劇（farce），不值得從喜劇的角度認真看待。英國詩人及評論家柯立芝（Samuel Taylor Coleridge）就曾經說過，雙胞胎的角色勉強維持了喜劇的主題，但增加另一對雙胞胎卻是劇作家與觀眾雙方同意的協定：即使是最誇張的機緣巧合，也可以在劇場中成立。

劇中的某些情節也具有笑劇的特徵，例如兩人闊別多年後竟會在同一天穿上一模一樣的服裝，又例如被誤認的孿生子毆打僕人，被認為精神錯亂，而他則將誤會都歸咎於巫術。《牛津英語大辭典》中為笑劇所下的定義是：「通常為篇幅較短的戲劇作品，以引人發笑為唯一的目的。」

《連環錯》並不完全符合這個定義，因為劇中也有感人的情節，例如葉吉與雙胞胎兒子失散的苦難，男女的情愛，還有葉吉在最需要幫助時，親生兒子卻不認他。更重要的是，莎士比亞使葉吉籠罩在死亡的陰影下，直到劇終才得以解除，而死亡在多數的羅馬喜劇中向來都只是虛晃一招，沒有成真的可能。

席德尼爵士（Sir Philip Sidney）也說：「喜劇就是模仿生活中的誤會，用最滑稽可笑的方式呈現，使觀眾認為絕對不可能發生。」從這兩個角度來看，稱《連環錯》為喜劇並不為過。莎士比亞似乎在早期的劇場生涯就已經認為：歷經一連串的道德衝突或生命危險之後，最終達到圓滿結局，才算是喜劇收場。

宗教意喻

其實在羅馬喜劇的背後，隱約還帶有希臘風格。西元前四世紀末希臘新喜劇（New Comedy）的創始人米南德（Menander, 342–292 B.C.）及其他劇作家，似乎都最鍾愛錯認身分、和失散子女重逢等主題，或許是因為當時的政治經濟狀況混亂，使得和小孩離散成為司空見慣的事件。

隨著時空的推移，經過羅馬時期到伊莉莎白時期，莎士比亞又賦予這個傳統的戲劇文學新的活力與意義，並加入了基督教對大眾心理及道德價值的影響。《連環錯》的場景設在《聖經》中，聖保羅與使徒前往的以弗所，藉此將基督教思想注入劇本，呼應劇中人物的情緒和心理反應。例如葉吉最後出乎意料地無償獲得寬恕釋放，就是最好的例子，女修道院長也是基督徒的典範，而劇中對婚姻的描述建立在互愛與互敬之上，也吻合基督教思想。

雅卓安娜潑悍是因為懷疑丈夫不忠，丈夫因為妻子和別的男子吃飯，憤而去找其他女子，而露希安娜認為為人妻子應順從丈夫才是正道，其語氣和思想都類似莎士比亞同時期的喜劇《馴悍記》中改頭換面的凱薩琳，代表基督教對婚姻的典型觀點。

各種主題

劇中人物視周遭的人事物為理所當然，結果經由身分的錯置，使得他們能跳脫出原有觀點，重新審視生活中的大小事件。又待所有的混亂和誤解解除後，才恢復原有的秩序與理性，所有人的生活回歸正常。兩者的對比，如幻象與現實、瘋狂與理智，也是常見的莎劇主題。

在此劇，莎劇的另一個常見主題也有著墨：社會地位不平等的問題。一介平凡的商人無奈接受死刑，僕人遭主人毆打，諸如此類等等，都體現出此一問題。而在本劇中，作者並沒有允諾任何平等公義的力量，只展現出這種問題可以獲得解決，但本質仍然是無法改變的。

《連環錯》最早的演出紀錄是 1594 年 12 月 28 日，正值聖誕假期。三百年後，波爾（William Poel）將此劇重新搬上葛雷法律學院（Gray's Inn 或 the Honourable Society of Gray's Inn）的場地，旨在重現當時演出的風貌。這次演出讓人不得不承認《連環錯》在舞台上的確具有一定的戲劇效果，從此打破以往認為此劇過於粗俗、前後不相連貫的成見。時至今日，這齣戲仍然能夠引起許多觀眾（尤其是孩童）的笑聲及掌聲。

《連環錯》人物表

Aegeon	葉吉	溪洛窟的一位老商人
Antipholus	安提弗	葉吉的雙胞胎兒子，兄弟同名
Dromio	拙米歐	孿生奴僕，兄弟同名
Menaphon	梅納封公爵	以弗所的安提弗的養父
Adriana	雅卓安娜	以弗所的安提弗的妻子
Luciana	露希安娜	雅卓安娜的妹妹
lady abbess	修道院院長	葉吉失散多年的妻子

The Comedy of Errors

The states of Syracuse and Ephesus being at variance[1], there was a cruel law made at Ephesus, ordaining[2] that if any merchant of Syracuse was seen in the city of Ephesus, he was to be put to death, unless he could pay a thousand marks for the ransom[3] of his life.

Aegeon, an old merchant of Syracuse, was discovered in the streets of Ephesus, and brought before the duke, either to pay this heavy fine or to receive sentence of death.

Aegeon had no money to pay the fine, and the duke, before he pronounced the sentence of death upon him, desired him to relate the history of his life, and to tell for what cause he had ventured to come to the city of Ephesus, which it was death for any Syracusan merchant to enter.

1 variance ['veriəns] (n.) 意見不合；齟齬
2 ordain [ɔːr'deɪn] (v.) 命令；注定
3 ransom ['rænsəm] (n.) 贖金；贖回

Aegeon said that he did not fear to die, for sorrow had made him weary of his life, but that a heavier task could not have been imposed[4] upon him than to relate the events of his unfortunate life. He then began his own history, in the following words:

"I was born at Syracuse, and brought up to the profession of a merchant. I married a lady, with whom I lived very happily, but, being obliged to go to Epidamnum, I was detained there by my business six months, and then, finding I should be obliged to stay some time longer, I sent for my wife, who, as soon as she arrived, was brought to bed of two sons, and what was very strange, they were both so exactly alike that it was impossible to distinguish the one from the other.

"At the same time that my wife was brought to bed of these twin boys, a poor woman in the inn where my wife lodged was brought to bed of two sons, and these twins were as much like each other as my two sons were. The parents of these children being exceeding poor, I bought the two boys and brought them up to attend upon my sons.

4 impose [ɪm'pouz] (v.) 徵……；加於

"My sons were very fine children, and my wife was not a little proud of two such boys; and she daily wishing to return home, I unwillingly agreed, and in an evil hour we got on shipboard, for we had not sailed above a league from Epidamnum before a dreadful storm arose, which continued with such violence that the sailors, seeing no chance of saving the ship, crowded into the boat to save their own lives, leaving us alone in the ship, which we every moment expected would be destroyed by the fury of the storm.

"The incessant[5] weeping of my wife and the piteous complaints of the pretty babes, who, not knowing what to fear, wept for fashion, because they saw their mother weep, filled me with terror for them, though I did not for myself fear death; and all my thoughts were bent to contrive[6] means for their safety. I tied my youngest son to the end of a small spare mast, such as seafaring men provide against storms; at the other end I bound the youngest of the twin slaves, and at the same time I directed my wife how to fasten the other children in like manner to another mast.

5 incessant [ɪnˈsesənt] (a.) 不斷的；不停的
6 contrive [kənˈtraɪv] (v.) 設計；想辦法

"She thus having the care of the two eldest children, and I of the two younger, we bound ourselves separately to these masts with the children; and but for this contrivance we had all been lost, for the ship split on a mighty rock and was dashed in pieces; and we, clinging to these slender masts, were supported above the water, where I, having the care of two children, was unable to assist my wife, who, with the other children, was soon separated from me; but while they were yet in my sight, they were taken up by a boat of fishermen, from Corinth (as I supposed), and, seeing them in safety.

"I had no care but to struggle with the wild sea-waves, to preserve my dear son and the youngest slave. At length we, in our turn, were taken up by a ship, and the sailors, knowing me, gave us kind welcome and assistance and landed us in safety at Syracuse; but from that sad hour I have never known what became of my wife and eldest child.

"My youngest son, and now my only care, when he was eighteen years of age, began to be inquisitive[7] after his mother and his brother, and often importuned[8] me that he might take his attendant, the young slave, who had also lost his brother, and go in search of them. At length I unwillingly gave consent, for, though I anxiously desired to hear tidings of my wife and eldest son, yet in sending my younger one to find them, I hazarded the loss of him also.

"It is now seven years since my son left me; five years have I passed in traveling through the world in search of him. I have been in farthest Greece, and through the bounds of Asia, and, coasting homewards, I landed here in Ephesus, being unwilling to leave any place unsought that harbors men; but this day must end the story of my life, and happy should I think myself in my death if I were assured my wife and sons were living."

---

7 inquisitive [ɪnˈkwɪzɪtɪv] (a.) 好管閒事的
8 importune [ˌɪmpərˈtuːn] (v.) 再三請求

Here the hapless[9] Aegeon ended the account of his misfortunes; and the duke, pitying this unfortunate father who had brought upon himself this great peril by his love for his lost son, said if it were not against the laws, which his oath and dignity did not permit him to alter, he would freely pardon him; yet, instead of dooming him to instant death, as the strict letter of the law required, he would give him that day to try if he could beg or borrow the money to pay the fine.

This day of grace did seem no great favor to Aegeon, for, not knowing any man in Ephesus, there seemed to him but little chance that any stranger would lend or give him a thousand marks to pay the fine; and, helpless and hopeless of any relief, he retired from the presence of the duke in the custody[10] of a jailor.

Aegeon supposed he knew no person in Ephesus; but at the very time he was in danger of losing his life through the careful search he was making after his youngest son, that son, and his eldest son also, were both in the city of Ephesus.

---

9 hapless ['hæpləs] (a.) 不幸的
10 custody ['kʌstədi] (n.) 監禁

Aegeon's sons, besides being exactly alike in face and person, were both named alike, being both called Antipholus, and the two twin slaves were also both named Dromio. Aegeon's youngest son, Antipholus of Syracuse, he whom the old man had come to Ephesus to seek, happened to arrive at Ephesus with his slave Dromio that very same day that Aegeon did; and he being also a merchant of Syracuse, he would have been in the same danger that his father was, but by good fortune he met a friend who told him the peril an old merchant of Syracuse was in, and advised him to pass for a merchant of Epidamnum. This Antipholus agreed to do, and he was sorry to hear one of his own countrymen was in this danger, but he little thought this old merchant was his own father.

The eldest son of Aegeon (who must be called Antipholus of Ephesus, to distinguish him from his brother Antipholus of Syracuse) had lived at Ephesus twenty years, and, being a rich man, was well able to have paid the money for the ransom of his father's life; but Antipholus knew nothing of his father, being so young when he was taken out of the sea with his mother by the fishermen that he only remembered he had been so preserved; but he had no recollection of either his father or his mother, the fishermen who took up this Antipholus and his mother and the young slave Dromio, having carried the two children away from her (to the great grief of that unhappy lady), intending to sell them.

Antipholus and Dromio were sold by them to Duke Menaphon, a famous warrior, who was uncle to the Duke of Ephesus, and he carried the boys to Ephesus when he went to visit the duke, his nephew.

The Duke of Ephesus, taking a liking to young Antipholus, when he grew up, made him an officer in his army, in which he distinguished himself by his great bravery in the wars, where he saved the life of his patron, the duke, who rewarded his merit by marrying him to Adriana, a rich lady of Ephesus, with whom he was living (his slave Dromio still attending him) at the time his father came there.

Antipholus of Syracuse, when he parted with his friend, who, advised him to say he came from Epidamnum, gave his slave Dromio some money to carry to the inn where he intended to dine, and in the mean time he said he would walk about and view the city and observe the manners of the people.

Dromio was a pleasant fellow, and when Antipholus was dull and melancholy he used to divert[11] himself with the odd humors and merry jests of his slave, so that the freedoms of speech he allowed in Dromio were greater than is usual between masters and their servants.

---

11 divert [daɪˈvɜːrt] (v.) 娛樂；款待

When Antipholus of Syracuse had sent Dromio away, he stood awhile thinking over his solitary[12] wanderings in search of his mother and his brother, of whom in no place where he landed could he hear the least tidings; and he said sorrowfully to himself, "I am like a drop of water in the ocean, which, seeking to find its fellow drop, loses itself in the wide sea. So I, unhappily, to find a mother and a brother, do lose myself."

While he was thus meditating on his weary travels, which had hitherto been so useless, Dromio (as he thought) returned. Antipholus, wondering that he came back so soon, asked him where he had left the money. Now it was not his own Dromio, but the twin-brother that lived with Antipholus of Ephesus, that he spoke to. The two Dromios and the two Antipholuses were still as much alike as Aegeon had said they were in their infancy[13]; therefore no wonder Antipholus thought it was his own slave returned, and asked him why he came back so soon.

---

12 solitary ['sɔːləteri] (a.) 單獨的
13 infancy ['ɪnfənsi] (n.) 嬰兒期；幼兒

Dromio replied: "My mistress sent me to bid you come to dinner. The capon[14] burns, and the pig falls from the spit[15], and the meat will be all cold if you do not come home."

"These jests are out of season," said Antipholus. "Where did you leave the money?"

"Dromio still answering that his mistress had sent him to fetch Antipholus to dinner, "What mistress?" said Antipholus.

"Why, your worship's wife, sir!" replied Dromio.

Antipholus having no wife, he was very angry with Dromio, and said: "Because I familiarly sometimes chat with you, you presume[16] to jest with me in this free manner. I am not in a sportive humor now. Where is the money? We being strangers here, how dare you trust so great a charge from your own custody?"

Dromio, hearing his master, as he thought him, talk of their being strangers, supposing Antipholus was jesting, replied, merrily: "I pray you, sir, jest as you sit at dinner. I had no charge but to fetch you home to dine with my mistress and her sister."

14 capon ['keɪpən] (n.) 閹雞

15 spit [spɪt] (n.) 烤肉叉

16 presume [prɪ'zuːm] (v.) 擅敢；冒昧

◄42► Now Antipholus lost all patience, and beat Dromio, who ran home and told his mistress that his master had refused to come to dinner and said that he had no wife.

Adriana, the wife of Antipholus of Ephesus, was very angry when she heard that her husband said he had no wife; for she was of a jealous temper, and she said her husband meant that he loved another lady better than herself; and she began to fret[17], and say unkind words of jealousy and reproach of her husband; and her sister Luciana, who lived with her, tried in vain to persuade her out of her groundless suspicions.

Antipholus of Syracuse went to the inn, and found Dromio with the money in safety there, and, seeing his own Dromio, he was going again to chide[18] him for his free jests, when Adriana came up to him, and, not doubting but it was her husband she saw, she began to reproach him for looking strange upon her (as well he might, never having seen this angry lady before); and then she told him how well he loved her before they were married, and that now he loved some other lady instead of her.

17 fret [frɛt] (v.) 煩惱；不滿；煩躁
18 chide [tʃaɪd] (v.) 責怪；斥責

"How comes it now, my husband," said she, "oh, how comes it that I have lost your love?"

"Plead you to me, fair dame?" said the astonished Antipholus.

It was in vain he told her he was not her husband and that he had been in Ephesus but two hours. She insisted on his going home with her, and Antipholus at last, being unable to get away, went with her to his brother's house, and dined with Adriana and her sister, the one calling him husband and the other brother, he, all amazed, thinking he must have been married to her in his sleep, or that he was sleeping now. And Dromio, who followed them, was no less surprised, for the cook-maid, who was his brother's wife, also claimed him for her husband.

While Antipholus of Syracuse was dining with his brother's wife, his brother, the real husband, returned home to dinner with his slave Dromio; but the servants would not open the door, because their mistress had ordered them not to admit any company; and when they repeatedly knocked, and said they were

Antipholus and Dromio, the maids laughed at them, and said that Antipholus was at dinner with their mistress, and Dromio was in the kitchen, and though they almost knocked the door down, they could not gain admittance, and at last Antipholus went away very angry, and strangely surprised at, hearing a gentleman was dining with his wife.

When Antipholus of Syracuse had finished his dinner, he was so perplexed[19] at the lady's still persisting in calling him husband, and at hearing that Dromio had also been claimed by the cookmaid, that he left the house as soon as he could find any pretence[20] to get away; for though he was very much pleased with Luciana, the sister, yet the jealous-tempered Adriana he disliked very much, nor was Dromio at all better satisfied with his fair wife in the kitchen; therefore both master and man were glad to get away from their new wives as fast as they could.

---

19 perplexed [pər'plekst] (a.) 困惑的
20 pretence ['priːtens] (n.) 藉口；託辭

The moment Antipholus of Syracuse had left the house he was met by a goldsmith, who, mistaking him, as Adriana had done, for Antipholus of Ephesus, gave him a gold chain, calling him by his name; and when Antipholus would have refused the chain, saying it did not belong to him, the goldsmith replied he made it by his own orders, and went away, leaving the chain in the hands of Antipholus, who ordered his man Dromio to get his things on board a ship, not choosing to stay in a place any longer where he met with such strange adventures that he surely thought himself bewitched[21].

The goldsmith who had given the chain to the wrong Antipholus was arrested immediately after for a sum of money he owed; and Antipholus, the married brother, to whom the goldsmith thought he had given the chain, happened to come to the place where the officer was arresting the goldsmith, who, when he saw Antipholus, asked him to pay for the gold chain he had just delivered to him, the price amounting to nearly the same sum as that for which he had been arrested.

---

21 bewitched [bɪ'wɪtʃt] (a.) 中邪的

Antipholus denying the having received the chain, and the goldsmith persisting to declare that he had but a few minutes before given it to him, they disputed this matter a long time, both thinking they were right; for Antipholus knew the goldsmith never gave him the chain, and so like were the two brothers, the goldsmith was as certain he had delivered the chain into his hands, till at last the officer took the goldsmith away to prison for the debt he owed, and at the same time the goldsmith made the officer arrest Antipholus for the price of the chain; so that at the conclusion of their dispute, Antipholus and the merchant were both taken away to prison together.

As Antipholus was going to prison, he met Dromio of Syracuse, his brother's slave, and, mistaking him for his own, he ordered him to go to Adriana his wife, and tell her to send the money for which he was arrested.

Dromio, wondering that his master should send him back to the strange house where he dined, and from which he had just before been in such haste to depart, did not dare to reply, though he came to tell his master the ship was ready to sail, for he saw Antipholus was in no humor to be jested with. Therefore he went away, grumbling within himself that he must return to Adriana's house, "Where," said he, "Dowsabel claims me for a husband. But I must go, for servants must obey their masters' commands."

Adriana gave him the money, and as Dromio was returning he met Antipholus of Syracuse, who was still in amaze at the surprising adventures he met with, for his brother being well known in Ephesus, there was hardly a man he met in the streets but saluted him as an old acquaintance. Some offered him money which they said was owing to him, some invited him to come and see them, and some gave him thanks for kindnesses they said he had done them, all mistaking him for his brother. A tailor showed him some silks he had bought for him, and insisted upon taking measure of him for some clothes.

Antipholus began to think he was among a nation of sorcerers[22] and witches, and Dromio did not at all relieve his master from his bewildered[23] thoughts by asking him how he got free from the officer who was carrying him to prison, and giving him the purse of gold which Adriana had sent to pay the debt with.

---

22 sorcerer ['sɔːrsərər] (n.) 魔法師；術士；男巫師
23 bewildered [bɪ'wɪldərd] (a.) 迷惑的；中邪的

This talk of Dromio's of the arrest and of a prison, and of the money he had brought from Adriana, perfectly confounded Antipholus, and he said, "This fellow Dromio is certainly distracted[24], and we wander here in illusions," and, quite terrified at his own confused thoughts, he cried out, "Some blessed power deliver us from this strange place!"

And now another stranger came up to him, and she was a lady, and she, too, called him Antipholus, and told him he had dined with her that day, and asked him for a gold chain which she said he had promised to give her.

Antipholus now lost all patience, and, calling her a sorceress, he denied that he had ever promised her a chain, or dined with her, or had even seen her face before that moment. The lady persisted in affirming he had dined with her and had promised her a chain, which Antipholus still denying, she further said that she had given him a valuable ring, and if he would not give her the gold chain, she insisted upon having her own ring again.

---

24 distracted [dɪ'stræktɪd] (a.) 心情紛亂的

On this Antipholus became quite frantic[25], and again calling her sorceress and witch, and denying all knowledge of her or her ring, ran away from her, leaving her astonished at his words and his wild looks, for nothing to her appeared more certain than that he had dined with her, and that she had given him a ring in consequence of his promising to make her a present of a gold chain. But this lady had fallen into the same mistake the others had done, for she had taken him for his brother; the married Antipholus had done all the things she taxed this Antipholus with.

When the married Antipholus was denied entrance into his house (those within supposing him to be already there), he had gone away very angry, believing it to be one of his wife's jealous freaks, to which she was very subject, and, remembering that she had often falsely accused him of visiting other ladies, he, to be revenged on her for shutting him out of his own house, determined to go and dine with this lady, and she receiving him with great civility, and his wife having so highly offended him, Antipholus promised to give her a gold chain which he had intended as a present for his wife; it was the same chain which the goldsmith by mistake had given to his brother.

25 frantic ['fræntɪk] (a.) 狂亂的

The lady liked so well the thoughts of having a fine gold chain that she gave the married Antipholus a ring; which when, as she supposed (taking his brother for him), he denied, and said he did not know her, and left her in such a wild passion, she began to think he was certainly out of his senses; and presently she resolved to go and tell Adriana that her husband was mad.

And while she was telling it to Adriana, he came, attended by the jailor (who allowed him to come home to get the money to pay the debt), for the purse of money which Adriana had sent by Dromio and he had delivered to the other Antipholus.

Adriana believed the story the lady told her of her husband's madness must be true when he reproached her for shutting him out of his own house; and remembering how he had protested all dinner-time that he was not her husband and had never been in Ephesus till that day, she had no doubt that he was mad; she therefore paid the jailor the money, and, having discharged him, she ordered her servants to bind her husband with ropes, and had him conveyed into a dark room, and sent for a doctor to come and cure him of his madness, Antipholus all the while hotly exclaiming against this false accusation, which the exact likeness he bore to his brother had brought upon him. But his rage only the more confirmed them in the belief that he was mad; and Dromio persisting in the same story, they bound him also and took him away along with his master.

Soon after Adriana had put her husband into confinement[26] a servant came to tell her that Antipholus and Dromio must have broken loose from their keepers, for that they were both walking at liberty in the next street.

On hearing this, Adriana ran out to fetch him home, taking some people with her to secure her husband again; and her sister went along with her.

When they came to the gates of a convent[27] in their neighborhood, there they saw Antipholus and Dromio, as they thought, being again deceived by the likeness of the twin brothers.

---

26 confinement [kən'faɪnmənt] (n.) 限制；監禁
27 convent ['kɑːnvənt] (n.) 女修道院

Antipholus of Syracuse was still beset with the perplexities this likeness had brought upon him. The chain which the goldsmith had given him was about his neck, and the goldsmith was reproaching him for denying that he had it and refusing to pay for it, and Antipholus was protesting that the goldsmith freely gave him the chain in the morning, and that from that hour he had never seen the goldsmith again.

And now Adriana came up to him and claimed him as her lunatic husband who had escaped from his keepers, and the men she brought with her were going to lay violent hands on Antipholus and Dromio; but they ran into the convent, and Antipholus begged the abbess[28] to give him shelter in her house.

And now came out the lady abbess herself to inquire into the cause of this disturbance. She was a grave and venerable lady, and wise to judge of what she saw, and she would not too hastily give up the man who had sought protection in her house; so she strictly questioned the wife about the story she told of her husband's madness, and she said: "What is the cause of this sudden distemper[29] of your husband's? Has he lost his wealth at sea? Or is it the death of some dear friend that has disturbed his mind?"

28 abbess ['æbɪs] (n.) 女修道院院長
29 distemper [dɪ'stempər] (n.) 思緒混亂

🎧 50 Adriana replied that no such things as these had been the cause.

"Perhaps," said the abbess, "he has fixed his affections on some other lady than you, his wife, and that has driven him to this state."

Adriana said she had long thought the love of some other lady was the cause of his frequent absences from home.

Now it was not his love for another, but the teasing jealousy of his wife's temper, that often obliged Antipholus to leave his home; and the abbess (suspecting this from the vehemence[30] of Adriana's manner), to learn the truth, said: "You should have reprehended[31] him for this."

"Why, so I did," replied Adriana.

"Aye," said the abbess, "but perhaps not enough."

Adriana, willing to convince the abbess that she had said enough to Antipholus on this subject, replied: "It was the constant subject of our conversation; in bed I would not let him sleep for speaking of it. At table I would not let him eat for speaking of it. When

I was alone with him I talked of nothing else; and in company I gave him frequent hints of it. Still all my talk was how vile[32] and bad it was in him to love any lady better than me."

The lady abbess, having drawn this full confession from the jealous Adriana, now said: "And therefore comes it that your husband is mad. The venomous[33] clamor[34] of a jealous woman is a more deadly poison than a mad dog's tooth. It seems his sleep was hindered by your railing; no wonder that his head is light; and his meat was sauced with your upbraidings[35]; unquiet meals make ill digestions, and that has thrown him into this fever. You say his sports were disturbed by your brawls[36]; being debarred[37] from the enjoyment of society and recreation, what could ensue but dull melancholy and comfortless despair? The consequence is, then, that your jealous fits have made your husband mad."

---

30 vehemence ['viːməns] (n.) 激動；憤怒；猛烈
31 reprehend [ˌreprɪ'hend] (v.) 責難；譴責
32 vile [vaɪl] (a.) 卑鄙的
33 venomous ['venəməs] (a.) 惡毒的
34 clamor ['klæmər] (n.) 喧鬧
35 upbraiding [ʌp'breɪdɪŋ] (n.) 斥責；譴責
36 brawl [brɔːl] (n.) 大聲的爭吵
37 debar [dɪ'bɑːr] (v.) 排除

Luciana would have excused her sister, saying she always reprehended her husband mildly; and she said to her sister, "Why do you hear these rebukes[38] without answering them?"

But the abbess had made her so plainly perceive her fault that she could only answer, "She has betrayed me to my own reproof[39]."

Adriana, though ashamed of her own conduct, still insisted on having her husband delivered up to her; but the abbess would suffer no person to enter her house, nor would she deliver up this unhappy man to the care of the jealous wife, determining herself to use gentle means for his recovery, and she retired into her house again, and ordered her gates to be shut against them.

During the course of this eventful day, in which so many errors had happened from the likeness the twin brothers bore to each other, old Aegeon's day of grace was passing away, it being now near sunset; and at sunset he was doomed to die if he could not pay the money.

---

38 rebuke [rɪ'bjuːk] (n.) 指責
39 reproof [rɪ'pruːf] (n.) 譴責；非難

The place of his execution was near this convent, and here he arrived just as the abbess retired into the convent; the duke attending in person, that, if any offered to pay the money, he might be present to pardon him.

Adriana stopped this melancholy procession, and cried out to the duke for justice, telling him that the abbess had refused to deliver up her lunatic[40] husband to her care. While she was speaking, her real husband and his servant, Dromio, who had got loose, came before the duke to demand justice, complaining that his wife had confined him on a false charge of lunacy, and telling in what manner he had broken his bands and eluded[41] the vigilance[42] of his keepers.

Adriana was strangely surprised to see her husband when she thought he had been within the convent.

40 lunatic ['luːnətɪk] (a.) 瘋的；精神錯亂的
41 elude [ɪ'luːd] (v.) 逃避
42 vigilance ['vɪdʒɪləns] (n.) 留心；警戒

Aegeon, seeing his son, concluded this was the son who had left him to go in search of his mother and his brother, and he felt secure that this dear son would readily pay the money demanded for his ransom. He therefore spoke to Antipholus in words of fatherly affection, with joyful hope that he should now be released.

But, to the utter astonishment of Aegeon, his son denied all knowledge of him, as well he might, for this Antipholus had never seen his father since they were separated in the storm in his infancy. But while the poor old Aegeon was in vain endeavoring to make his son acknowledge him, thinking surely that either his griefs and the anxieties he had suffered had so strangely altered him that his son did not know him or else that he was ashamed to acknowledge his father in his misery—in the midst of this perplexity, the lady abbess and the other Antipholus and Dromio came out, and the wondering Adriana saw two husbands and two Dromios standing before her.

And now these riddling errors, which had so perplexed them all, were clearly made out. When the duke saw the two Antipholuses and the two Dromios both so exactly alike, he at once conjectured[43] aright of these seeming mysteries, for he remembered the story Aegeon had told him in the morning; and he said these men must be the two sons of Aegeon and their twin slaves.

---

43 conjecture [kən'dʒektʃər] (v.) 推測；猜測

But now an unlooked-for joy indeed completed the history of Aegeon; and the tale he had in the morning told in sorrow, and under sentence of death, before the setting sun went down was brought to a happy conclusion, for the venerable lady abbess made herself known to be the long-lost wife of Aegeon and the fond mother of the two Antipholuses.

When the fishermen took the eldest Antipholus and Dromio away from her, she entered a nunnery, and by her wise and virtuous conduct she was at length made lady abbess of this convent and in discharging the rites of hospitality to an unhappy stranger she had unknowingly protected her own son.

Joyful congratulations and affectionate greetings between these long-separated parents and their children made them for a while forget that Aegeon was yet under sentence of death. But when they were become a little calm, Antipholus of Ephesus offered the duke the ransom money for his father's life; but the duke freely pardoned Aegeon, and would not take the money.

And the duke went with the abbess and her newly found husband and children into the convent, to hear this happy family discourse at leisure of the blessed ending of their adverse[44] fortunes. And the two Dromios' humble joy must not be forgotten; they had their congratulations and greetings, too, and each Dromio pleasantly complimented his brother on his good looks, being well pleased to see his own person (as in a glass) show so handsome in his brother.

Adriana had so well profited by the good counsel of her mother-in-law that she never after cherished unjust suspicions or was jealous of her husband.

Antipholus of Syracuse married the fair Luciana, the sister of his brother's wife; and the good old Aegeon, with his wife and sons, lived at Ephesus many years. Nor did the unraveling of these perplexities so entirely remove every ground of mistake for the future but that sometimes, to remind them of adventures past, comical blunders would happen, and the one Antipholus, and the one Dromio, be mistaken for the other, making altogether a pleasant and diverting Comedy of Errors.

---

44 adverse ['ædvɜːrs] (a.) 不利的；反對的

《連環錯》名句選

Dromio	But I pray, sir, why am I beaten?
Antipholus	Dost thou not know?
Dromio	Nothing, sir, but that I am beaten.
Antipholus	Shall I tell you why?
Dromio	Ay, sir, and wherefore; for they say, every why hath a wherefore.
Antipholus	Why, first, for flouting me, and then wherefore, for urging it the second time to me.
Dromio	Was there ever any man thus beaten out of season, When in the why and the wherefore is neither rhyme nor reason?

(II, ii, 39–48)

拙米歐　少爺，我為什麼要挨打？

安提弗　你不知道嗎？

拙米歐　少爺，我不知道，我只知道我挨打了。

安提弗　要我告訴你理由嗎？

拙米歐　是，少爺，還有原因，因為俗話說得好，
　　　　理出必有因。

安提弗　先說理由，你頂撞我，再說原因，
　　　　還逼問我為什麼。

拙米歐　真倒楣，白白挨了這一頓拳腳，
　　　　理由和原因卻還是莫名其妙。

　　　　(第二幕，第二景，39-48行)

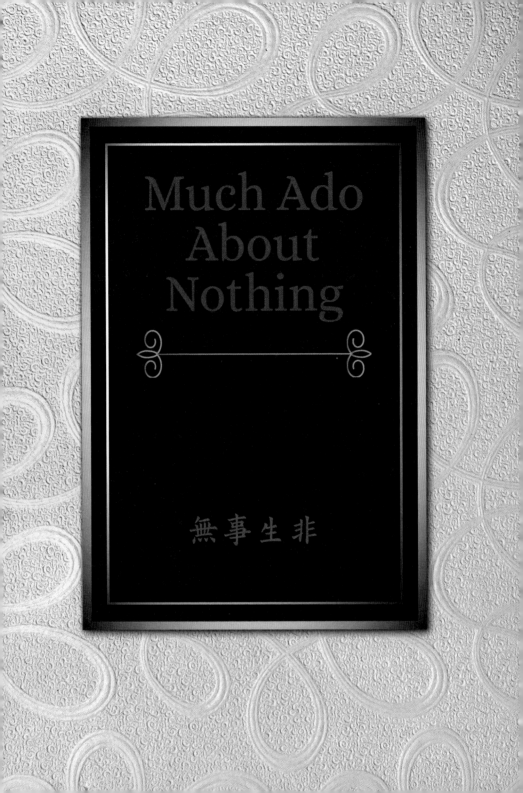

Much Ado About Nothing

無事生非

《無事生非》導讀

真實生活中的喜劇

《無事生非》寫作年代應在 1598–1599 年，是莎士比亞喜劇寫作最成熟時期的創作，內容熱鬧歡樂，富有哲思。故事主旨為面具、偽裝或遊戲，劇中人物探尋的則是男女關係中的自我意識以及真誠與尊重。

在伊莉莎白時期的英國，「無事」（nothing）的發音與 noting 極為類似，因此「無事生非」也有「注意」、「紀錄」、「竊聽生非」的雙關語暗示。「竊聽」在劇中不僅常見，而且至關重要，是造成誤解或澄清事實的關鍵。

比起莎士比亞的其他喜劇，例如《連環錯》、《仲夏夜之夢》、《皆大歡喜》、《第十二夜》等，本劇的特徵是場景和語言較為接近真實生活。《無》劇沒有脫離現實的浪漫場景，而是在梅西納城；劇中人並非一見鍾情，而是從相識的友人開始；本劇語言也不像極度浪漫的詩文，而是當時的一般口語。諸如此類的安排，使得本劇真實性高，彷彿是一般人也會發生的故事。

劇情架構

劇中的架構主要由兩對情侶所組成。希柔和碧翠絲是情同手足的表姊妹，克勞迪和班狄克是親王唐沛左的好友，四人雙雙演出兩種截然不同的愛情。希柔優雅沉靜，克勞迪叱吒戰場，兩人代表傳統的結合。碧翠絲和班狄克之間則是永無休止的唇槍舌戰，儘管最終配對成功，但兩人都仍堅持戴著原本尖酸嘲諷的面具。

這兩條故事線，是莎士比亞取材不同故事改編而成。希柔和克勞迪的故事似乎是根據義大利的亞瑞歐托（Ariosto）在 1516 年出版的《瘋狂奧蘭多》（*Orlando Furioso*），以及邦代羅（Matteo Bandello）於 1554 年出版的《小說》（*Novella*）中的第二十二個短篇小說所改寫而成。這則含悲劇成分的故事，帶有浪漫多情的義大利風味。此外，在文藝復興時期，時而可見未婚女子被污衊的題材，其中也有不少以悲劇作收，在史賓賽（Edmund Spenser）的《仙后》（*Faerie Queene*）中就有類似的例子。

碧翠絲與班狄克

碧翠絲與班狄克的故事源自英式幽默。在中古時期的英國，兩性戰爭是個常見的主題，喬叟（Geoffrey Chaucer）和韋克非（Wakefield）都寫過這類故事。莎士比亞早期的《馴悍記》也是類似的題材，凱瑟琳和皮楚丘最初充滿敵意，互相羞辱和攻擊，最後卻彼此傾心。碧翠絲和班狄克的故事很成功，為英國的喜劇文學立下良好典範，王爾德（Oscar Wilde）和蕭伯納（George Bernard Shaw）都是後來的佼佼者。

兩段感情的發展呈現不同的本質。碧翠絲和班狄克這兩個角色的心理層面較為複雜，他們都是自我意識很強的人，對伴侶的要求也高。然而這種生活態度往往和真實情感相左，因此需要旁人相助來讓兩人卸下高傲的面具。另外，兩人都是在偷聽到友人的談話之後才知道自己的毛病，但都誠懇地接受批評，並放下身段接受被設計而來的感情。

1861 年，白遼士（Hector Louis Berlioz）將此劇改編為歌劇，並改名為《碧翠絲與班狄克》（*Beatrice et Benedict*），無數的演員、觀眾和讀者都能認同，但兩人的戀情無法自成一個劇本，因為碧翠絲如果不要求班狄克去殺克勞迪，就無法顯示班狄克在舊友與新歡之間的為難與衝突，也無法證明他對愛情的承諾。

傳統對女性的要求

相形之下，希柔和克勞迪的故事就顯得平板單調，因而往往被視為次要角色。希柔溫馴聽話，不像希臘神話裡的希柔，為愛打破宗教誓約，甚至犧牲性命。克勞迪對他和希柔的婚事很慎重，他請求親王作媒，在確定希柔和她父親都同意了之後才安心。這段姻緣理性而有計畫，一切遵循社會規範與門第觀念。

克勞迪冤枉希柔，看似是一場「無事生非」的誤會，但那種慘痛經驗卻是劇中人的試煉。碧翠絲和修道士深信希柔清白無辜，班狄克儘管內心掙扎，但也通過了碧翠絲的考驗。克勞迪輕易拒絕並羞辱所愛的女子，暴露了對自己和對希柔的無知，因此這場誤會並不能完全歸咎於為非作歹的唐降。

希柔的父親李歐拿多一聽到他人對女兒的指控，馬上信以為真，以為女兒做出不名譽的事，又為確保女兒對未來夫婿忠貞不二，甚至寧願她就此死去。克勞迪、親王和李歐拿多的反應，反映了男人對女人不忠的深刻恐懼。

在莎士比亞的喜劇中，幾乎都是在與死神錯身而過之後，才得到圓滿結果，例如早期的《連環錯》、《仲夏夜之夢》和後來的《皆大歡喜》等。但與《威尼斯商人》和《一報還一報》相較之下，本劇中的死亡威脅就顯得毫不緊迫。

私生子唐降和《奧塞羅》中的以阿苟一樣邪惡，善於利用人們不可靠的視覺和聽覺來誤導仇人。但他陷害希柔並不是為了求什麼好處，只不過是想惱怒親王兄長，讓親王和親王周遭的人都變得和他自己一樣陰鬱罷了。劇中對唐降這個角色的心理、性格和背景並未加以著墨，故只能說是為了阻礙喜劇收場的一項安排。

《無事生非》人物表

Hero	希柔	和碧翠絲是表姐妹，後來與克勞迪結婚
Beatrice	碧翠絲	個性活潑，和班狄克是歡喜冤家
Leonato	李歐拿多	梅西納的總督，希柔的父親
Don Pedro	唐沛左	親王，想撮合碧翠絲和班狄克
Claudio	克勞迪	貴族，親王的友人
Benedick	班狄克	貴族，親王的友人
Ursula	烏蘇拉	總督的侍女
Margaret	瑪格莉特	總督的侍女
Don John	唐降	唐沛左同父異母的弟弟，想阻撓克勞迪和希柔的婚事
Borachio	包拉喬	被唐降收買，想破壞克勞迪的婚事

Much Ado About Nothing

[55] There lived in the palace at Messina two ladies, whose names were Hero and Beatrice. Hero was the daughter, and Beatrice the niece, of Leonato, the governor of Messina.

Beatrice was of a lively temper, and loved to divert[1] her cousin Hero, who was of a more serious disposition[2], with her sprightly sallies[3]. Whatever was going forward was sure to make matter of mirth[4] for the light-hearted Beatrice.

At the time the history of these ladies commences[5] some young men of high rank in the army, as they were passing through Messina on their return from a war that was just ended, in which they bad distinguished themselves by their great bravery, came to visit Leonato.

Beatrice

1 divert [daɪ'vɜːrt] (v.) 娛樂；消遣
2 disposition [ˌdɪspə'zɪʃən] (n.) 性質；氣質
3 sally ['sæli] (n.) 俏皮話；妙語
4 mirth [mɜːrθ] (n.) 歡樂
5 commence [kə'mens] (v.) 開始

Among these were Don Pedro, the Prince of Arragon; and his friend Claudio, who was a lord of Florence; and with them came the wild and witty Benedick, and he was a lord of Padua.

These strangers had been at Messina before, and the hospitable governor introduced them to his daughter and his niece as their old friends and acquaintance.

Benedick, the moment he entered the room, began a lively conversation with Leonato and the prince. Beatrice, who liked not to be left out of any discourse, interrupted Benedick with saying: "I wonder that you will still be talking, Signior Benedick. Nobody marks you."

Benedick was just such another rattlebrain[6] as Beatrice, yet he was not pleased at this free salutation, he thought it did not become a well-bred lady to be so flippant[7] with her tongue; and he remembered, when he was last at Messina, that Beatrice used to select him to make her merry jests upon.

---

6 rattlebrain ['rætl,breɪn] (n.) 輕率多話的人
7 flippant ['flɪpənt] (a.) 輕率的；無禮的

🎧 57 And as there is no one who so little likes to be made a jest of as those who are apt to take the same liberty themselves, so it was with Benedick and Beatrice; these two sharp wits never met in former times but a perfect war of raillery[8] was kept up between them, and they always parted mutually displeased with each other.

Therefore, when Beatrice stopped him in the middle of his discourse with telling him nobody marked what he was saying, Benedick, affecting not to have observed before that she was present, said, "What, my dear Lady Disdain, are you yet living?"

And now war broke out afresh between them, and a long jangling[9] argument ensued, during which Beatrice, although she knew he had so well approved his valor[10] in the late war, said that she would eat all he had killed there; and observing the prince take delight in Benedick's conversation, she called him "the prince's jester[11]." This sarcasm[12] sank deeper into the mind of Benedick than all Beatrice had said before.

---

8 raillery ['reɪlərɪ] (n.) 善意的嘲弄
9 jangling ['dʒæŋglɪŋ] (a.) 大聲吵架的
10 valor ['vælər] (n.) 勇敢
11 jester ['dʒestər] (n.) 弄臣
12 sarcasm ['sɑːrkæzəm] (n.) 譏諷語；挖苦話

The hint she gave him that he was a coward, by saying she would eat all he had killed, he did not regard, knowing himself to be a brave man; but there is nothing that great wits so much dread as the imputation[13] of buffoonery[14], because the charge comes sometimes a little too near the truth; therefore Benedick perfectly hated Beatrice when she called him "the prince's jester."

The modest lady Hero was silent before the noble guests; and while Claudio was attentively observing the improvement which time had made in her beauty, and was contemplating[15] the exquisite[16] graces of her fine figure (for she was an admirable young lady), the prince was highly amused with listening to the humorous dialogue between Benedick and Beatrice; and he said in a whisper to Leonato, "This is a pleasant-spirited young lady. She were an excellent wife for Benedick."

---

13 imputation [ˌɪmpjuˈteɪʃən] (n.) 歸咎；非難
14 buffoonery [bʌˈfuːnərɪ] (n.) 滑稽；詼諧
15 contemplate [ˈkɑːntemˌpleɪt] (v.) 注視
16 exquisite [ɪkˈskwɪzɪt] (a.) 優美的

58 Leonato replied to this suggestion, "O, my lord, my lord, if they were but a week married, they would talk themselves mad!"

But though Leonato thought they would make a discordant pair, the prince did not give up the idea of matching these two keen wits together.

When the prince returned with Claudio from the palace, he found that the marriage he had devised between Benedick and Beatrice was not the only one projected in that good company, for Claudio spoke in such terms of Hero, as made the prince guess at what was passing in his heart; and he liked it well, and he said to Claudio, "Do you affect Hero?"

To this question Claudio replied, "O, my lord, when I was last at Messina, I looked upon her with a soldier's eye, that liked, but had no leisure for loving; but now, in this happy time of peace, thoughts of war have left their places vacant in my mind, and in their room come thronging[17] soft and delicate thoughts, all prompting me how fair young Hero is, reminding me that I liked her before I went to the wars."

---

17 throng [θrɔːŋ] (v.) 聚集

🎧59 Claudio's confession of his love for Hero so wrought upon the prince, that he lost no time in soliciting[18] the consent of Leonato to accept of Claudio for a son-in-law.

Leonato agreed to this proposal, and the prince found no great difficulty in persuading the gentle Hero herself to listen to the suit of the noble Claudio, who was a lord of rare endowments[19], and highly accomplished, and Claudio, assisted by his kind prince, soon prevailed[20] upon Leonato to fix an early day for the celebration of his marriage with Hero.

Claudio was to wait but a few days before he was to be married to his fair lady; yet he complained of the interval being tedious, as indeed most young men are impatient when they are waiting for the accomplishment of any event they have set their hearts upon. The prince, therefore, to make the time seem short to him, proposed as a kind of merry pastime that they should invent some artful scheme to make Benedick and Beatrice fall in love with each other.

---

18 solicit [sə'lɪst] (v.) 懇求
19 endowment [ɪn'daʊmənt] (n.) 稟賦；才能
20 prevail [prɪ'veɪl] (v.) 勸說

Claudio entered with great satisfaction into this whim[21] of the prince, and Leonato promised them his assistance, and even Hero said she would do any modest office to help her cousin to a good husband.

The device the prince invented was that the gentlemen should make Benedick believe that Beatrice was in love with him, and that Hero should make Beatrice believe that Benedick was in love with her.

The prince, Leonato, and Claudio began their operations first; and watching upon an opportunity when Benedick was quietly seated reading in an arbor[22], the prince and his assistants took their station among the trees behind the arbor, so near that Benedick could not choose but hear all they said; and after some careless talk the prince said: "Come hither, Leonato. What was it you told me the other day—that your niece Beatrice was in love with Signior Benedick? I did never think that lady would have loved any man."

---

21 whim [wɪm] (n.) 突然的念頭；一時的興致
22 arbor ['ɑːrbər] (n.) 涼亭

"No, nor I neither, my lord," answered Leonato. "It is most wonderful that she should so dote[23] on Benedick, whom she in all outward behavior seemed ever to dislike."

Claudio confirmed all this with saying that Hero had told him Beatrice was so in love with Benedick, that she would certainly die of grief, if he could not be brought to love her; which Leonato and Claudio seemed to agree was impossible, he having always been such a railer against all fair ladies, and in particular against Beatrice.

The prince affected to hearken[24] to all this with great compassion for Beatrice, and he said, "It were good that Benedick were told of this."

"To what end?" said Claudio; "He would but make sport of it, and torment the poor lady worse."

"And if he should," said the prince, "it were a good deed to hang him; for Beatrice is an excellent sweet lady, and exceeding wise in everything but in loving Benedick."

Benedick in the Arbor

23 dote [doʊt] (v.) 鍾情
24 hearken [ˈhɑːrkən] (v.) 傾聽

Then the prince motioned to his companions that they should walk on, and leave Benedick to meditate upon what he had overheard.

Benedick had been listening with great eagerness to this conversation; and he said to himself when be heard Beatrice loved him, "Is it possible? Sits the wind in that corner?"

And when they were gone, he began to reason in this manner with himself: "This can be no trick! They were very serious, and they have the truth from Hero, and seem to pity the lady. Love me! Why, it must be requited[25]! I did never think to marry. But when I said I should die a bachelor, I did not think I should live to be married. They say the lady is virtuous and fair. She is so. And wise in everything but loving me. Why, that is no great argument of her folly. But here comes Beatrice. By this day, she is a fair lady. I do spy some marks of love in her."

Beatrice now approached him, and said with her usual tartness[26], "Against my will I am sent to bid you come in to dinner."

25 requite [rɪˈkwaɪt] (v.) 回報
26 tartness [ˈtɑːrtnɪs] (n.) 尖酸；辛辣

62

Benedick, who never felt himself disposed to speak so politely to her before, replied, "Fair Beatrice, I thank you for your pains."

And when Beatrice, after two or three more rude speeches, left him, Benedick thought he observed a concealed meaning of kindness under the uncivil words she uttered, and he said aloud, "If I do not take pity on her, I am a villain. If I do not love her, I am a Jew. I will go get her picture."

The gentleman being thus caught in the net they had spread for him, it was now Hero's turn to play her part with Beatrice; and for this purpose she sent for Ursula and Margaret, two gentlewomen who attended upon her, and she said to Margaret, "Good Margaret, run to the parlor; there you will find my cousin Beatrice talking with the prince and Claudio. Whisper in her ear, that I and Ursula are walking in the orchard, and that our discourse is all of her. Bid her steal into that pleasant arbor, where honeysuckles[27], ripened by the sun, like ungrateful minions[28], forbid the sun to enter."

27 honeysuckle [ˈhʌniˌsʌkəl] (n.) 忍冬；金銀花
28 minion [ˈmɪnjən] (n.) 寵僕

63

This arbor, into which Hero desired Margaret to entice[29] Beatrice, was the very same pleasant arbor where Benedick had so lately been an attentive listener.

"I will make her come, I warrant, presently," said Margaret.

Hero, then taking Ursula with her into the orchard, said to her, "Now, Ursula, when Beatrice comes, we will walk up and down this alley, and our talk must be only of Benedick, and when I name him, let it be your part to praise him more than ever man did merit. My talk to you must be how Benedick is in love with Beatrice. Now begin; for look where Beatrice like a lapwing[30] runs close by the ground, to hear our conference."

They then began, Hero saying, as if in answer to something which Ursula had said, "No, truly, Ursula. She is too disdainful; her spirits are as coy as wild birds of the rock."

29 entice [ɪnˈtaɪs] (v.) 誘使；慫恿
30 lapwing [ˈlæpˌwɪŋ] (n.) 田鳧；京燕

64

"But are you sure," said Ursula, "that Benedick loves Beatrice so entirely?"

Hero replied, "So says the prince, and my lord Claudio, and they entreated me to acquaint her with it; but I persuaded them, if they loved Benedick, never to let Beatrice know of it."

"Certainly," replied Ursula, "it were not good she knew his love, lest she made sport of it."

"Why, to say truth," said Hero, "I never yet saw a man, how wise soever, or noble, young, or rarely featured, but she would dispraise him."

"Sure, sure, such carping[31] is not commendable," said Ursula.

"No," replied Hero, "but who dare tell her so? If I should speak, she would mock me into air."

"Oh, you wrong your cousin!" said Ursula, "she cannot be so much without true judgment, as to refuse so rare a gentleman as Signior Benedick."

"He hath an excellent good name," said Hero. "indeed, he is the first man in Italy, always excepting my dear Claudio."

And now, Hero giving her attendant a hint that it was time to change the discourse, Ursula said, "And when are you to be married, madam?"

Hero then told her, that she was to be married to Claudio the next day, and desired she would go in with her, and look at some new attire[32], as she wished to consult with her on what she would wear on the morrow.

Beatrice, who had been listening with breathless eagerness to this dialogue, when they went away, exclaimed, "What fire is in mine ears? Can this be true? Farewell, contempt and scorn, and maiden pride, adieu! Benedick, love on! I will requite you, taming my wild heart to your loving hand."

31 carp [kɑːrp] (v.) 吹毛求疵
32 attire [əˈtaɪr] (n.) 服裝

65 It must have been a pleasant sight to see these old enemies converted[33] into new and loving friends, and to behold their first meeting after being cheated into mutual liking by the merry artifice of the good-humored prince. But a sad reverse in the fortunes of Hero must now be thought of. The morrow, which was to have been her wedding-day, brought sorrow on the heart of Hero and her good father, Leonato.

The prince had a half-brother, who came from the wars along with him to Messina. This brother (his name was Don John) was a melancholy, discontented man, whose spirits seemed to labor in the contriving of villainies.

He hated the prince his brother, and he hated Claudio, because he was the prince's friend, and determined to prevent Claudio's marriage with Hero, only for the malicious pleasure of making Claudio and the prince unhappy; for he knew the prince had set his heart upon this marriage, almost as much as Claudio himself; and to effect this wicked purpose, he employed one Borachio, a man as bad as himself, whom he encouraged with the offer of a great reward.

---

33 convert [kən'vɜːrt] (v.) 轉變

This Borachio paid his court to Margaret, Hero's attendant; and Don John, knowing this, prevailed upon him to make Margaret promise to talk with him from her lady's chamber window that night, after Hero was asleep, and also to dress herself in Hero's clothes, the better to deceive Claudio into the belief that it was Hero; for that was the end he meant to compass[34] by this wicked plot.

Don John then went to the prince and Claudio, and told them that Hero was an imprudent lady, and that she talked with men from her chamber window at midnight.

Now this was the evening before the wedding, and he offered to take them that night, where they should themselves hear Hero discoursing with a man from her window; and they consented to go along with him, and Claudio said, "If I see anything tonight why I should not marry her, tomorrow in the congregation[35], where I intended to wed her, there will I shame her."

---

34 compass ['kʌmpəs] (v.) 達到；獲得
35 congregation [ˌkɑːŋgrɪ'geɪʃən] (n.) 集合

The prince also said, "And as I assisted you to obtain her, I will join with you to disgrace her."

When Don John brought them near Hero's chamber that night, they saw Borachio standing under the window, and they saw Margaret looking out of Hero's window, and heard her talking with Borachio; and Margaret being dressed in the same clothes they had seen Hero wear, the prince and Claudio believed it was the lady Hero herself.

Nothing could equal the anger of Claudio, when he had made (as he thought) this discovery. All his love for the innocent Hero was at once converted into hatred, and he resolved to expose her in the church, as he had said he would, the next day; and the prince agreed to this, thinking no punishment could be too severe for the naughty lady, who talked with a man from her window the very night before she was going to be married to the noble Claudio.

67. The next day, when they were all met to celebrate the marriage, and Claudio and Hero were standing before the priest, and the priest, or friar, as he was called, was proceeding to pronounce the marriage ceremony, Claudio, in the most passionate language, proclaimed the guilt of the blameless Hero, who, amazed at the strange words he uttered, said, meekly, "Is my lord well, that he does speak so wide?"

Leonato, in the utmost horror, said to the prince, "My lord, why speak not you?"

"What should I speak?" said the prince, "I stand dishonored, that have gone about to link my dear friend to an unworthy woman. Leonato, upon my honor, myself, my brother, and this grieved Claudio, did see and bear her last night at midnight talk with a man at her chamber window."

Benedick in astonishment at what he heard, said, "This looks not like a nuptial."

68 "True, O God!" replied the heart-struck Hero; and then this hapless[36] lady sank down in a fainting fit, to all appearance dead.

The prince and Claudio left the church, without staying to see if Hero would recover, or at all regarding the distress into which they had thrown Leonato. So hard-hearted had their anger made them.

Benedick remained, and assisted Beatrice to recover Hero from her swoon[37], saying, "How does the lady?"

"Dead, I think," replied Beatrice in great agony[38] for she loved her cousin; and knowing her virtuous principles, she believed nothing of what she had heard spoken against her.

Not so the poor old father; he believed the story of his child's shame, and it was piteous to hear him lamenting over her, as she lay like one dead before him, wishing she might never more open her eyes.

But the ancient friar was a wise man, and full of observation on human nature, and he had attentively marked the lady's countenance[39] when she heard herself accused, and noted a thousand blushing shames to start into her face, and then he saw an angel-like whiteness bear away those blushes, and in her eye he saw a fire that did belie[40] the error that the prince did speak against her maiden truth, and he said to the sorrowing father, "Call me a fool; trust not my reading, nor my observation; trust not my age, my reverence, nor my calling, if this sweet lady lie not guiltless here under some biting error."

36 hapless ['hæpləs] (a.) 不幸的
37 swoon [swuːn] (n.) 昏厥
38 agony ['ægəni] (n.) 極大的痛苦
39 countenance ['kauntɪnəns] (n.) 面容
40 belie [bɪ'laɪ] (v.) 顯示……為虛假

69

When Hero had recovered from the swoon into which she had fallen, the friar said to her, "Lady, what man is he you are accused of?"

Hero replied, "They know that do accuse me; I know of none." Then turning to Leonato, she said, "O my father, if you can prove that any man has ever conversed with me at hours unmeet[41], or that I yesternight changed words with any creature, refuse me, hate me, torture me to death."

"There is," said the friar, "some strange misunderstanding in the prince and Claudio." And then he counseled Leonato, that he should report that Hero was dead; and he said that the deathlike swoon in which they had left Hero would make this easy of belief; and he also advised him that he should put on mourning, and erect a monument for her, and do all rites that appertain[42] to a burial.

"What shall become of this?" said Leonato. "What will this do?"

---

41 unmeet [ʌnˈmiːt] (a.) 不合適的
42 appertain [ˌæpərˈteɪn] (v.) 〔文學〕屬於

70

The friar replied, "This report of her death shall change slander[43] into pity; that is some good. But that is not all the good I hope for. When Claudio shall hear she died upon hearing his words, the idea of her life shall sweetly creep into his imagination. Then shall he mourn, if ever love had interest in his heart, and wish that he had not so accused her; yea, though he thought his accusation true."

Benedick now said, "Leonato, let the friar advise you; and though you know how well I love the prince and Claudio, yet on my honor I will not reveal this secret to them."

Leonato, thus persuaded, yielded; and he said sorrowfully, "I am so grieved, that the smallest twine[44] may lead me."

The kind friar then led Leonato and Hero away to comfort and console them, and Beatrice and Benedick remained alone; and this was the meeting from which their friends, who contrived[45] the merry plot against them, expected so much diversion[46]; those friends who were now overwhelmed with affliction[47], and from whose minds all thoughts of merriment seemed forever banished.

Benedick was the first who spoke, and he said, "Lady Beatrice, have you wept all this while?"

"Yea, and I will weep a while longer," said Beatrice.

"Surely," said Benedick, "I do believe your fair cousin is wronged."

"Ah," said Beatrice, "how much might that man deserve of me who would right her!"

Benedick then said, "Is there any way to show such friendship? I do love nothing in the world so well as you. Is not that strange?"

"It were as possible," said Beatrice, "for me to say I loved nothing in the world so well as you; but believe me not, and yet I lie not. I confess nothing, nor I deny nothing. I am sorry for my cousin."

"By my sword," said Benedick, "you love me, and I protest I love you. Come, bid me do anything for you."

---

43 slander ['slændər] (n.) 誹謗；詆毀；造謠中傷
44 twine [twaɪn] (n.) 細繩
45 contrive [kən'traɪv] (v.) 策畫
46 diversion [daɪ'vɜːrʒən] (n.) 轉向；改道
47 affliction [ə'flɪkʃən] (n.) 痛苦；苦難

BEATRICE. Talk with a man out at a window! A proper saying!
BENEDICK. Nay, but, Beatrice,--

Act. 4   Scene. 1

71 "Kill Claudio," said Beatrice.

"Ha! not for the wide world," said Benedick; for he loved his friend Claudio, and he believed he had been imposed[48] upon.

"Is not Claudio a villain, that has slandered, scorned, and dishonored my cousin?" said Beatrice, "oh, that I were a man!"

"Hear me, Beatrice!" said Benedick.

But Beatrice would hear nothing in Claudio's defense; and she continued to urge on Benedick to revenge her cousin's wrongs; and she said, "Talk with a man out of the window? a proper saying! Sweet Hero! she is wronged; she is slandered; she is undone. Oh, that I were a man for Claudio's sake! or that I had any friend, who would be a man for my sake! But valor is melted into courtesies and compliments. I cannot be a man with wishing, therefore I will die a woman with grieving."

"Tarry[49], good Beatrice," said Benedick, "by this hand I love you."

---

48 impose [ɪmˈpoʊz] (v.) 利用
49 tarry [ˈtæri] (v.) 停留

72 "Use it for my love some other way than swearing by it," said Beatrice.

"Think you on your soul that Claudio has wronged Hero?" asked Benedick.

"Yea," answered Beatrice; "as sure as I have a thought, or a soul."

"Enough," said Benedick. "I am engaged; I will challenge him. I will kiss your hand, and so leave you. By this hand, Claudio shall render me a dear account! As you hear from me, so think of me. Go, comfort your cousin."

While Beatrice was thus powerfully pleading with Benedick, and working his gallant[50] temper by the spirit of her angry words, to engage in the cause of Hero, and fight even with his dear friend Claudio, Leonato was challenging the prince and Claudio to answer with their swords the injury they had done his child, who, be affirmed, had died for grief. But they respected his age and his sorrow, and they said, "Nay, do not quarrel with us, good old man."

---

50 gallant [ˈɡælənt] (a.) 英勇的
51 magistrate [ˈmædʒɪstreɪt] (n.) 地方官吏

And now came Benedick, and he also challenged Claudio to answer with his sword the injury he had done to Hero; and Claudio and the prince said to each other, "Beatrice has set him on to do this."

Claudio, nevertheless, must have accepted this challenge of Benedick, had not the justice of heaven at the moment brought to pass a better proof of the innocence of Hero than the uncertain fortune of a duel.

While the prince and Claudio were yet talking of the challenge of Benedick, a magistrate[51] brought Borachio as a prisoner before the prince. Borachio had been overheard talking with one of his companions of the mischief he had been employed by Don John to do.

Borachio made a full confession to the prince in Claudio's hearing, that it was Margaret dressed in her lady's clothes that he had talked with from the window, whom they had mistaken for the lady Hero herself; and no doubt continued on the minds of Claudio and the prince of the innocence of Hero. If a suspicion had remained it must have been removed by the flight of Don John, who, finding his villainies were detected, fled from Messina to avoid the just anger of his brother.

🎧 73 The heart of Claudio was sorely grieved when he found he had falsely accused Hero, who, he thought, died upon hearing his cruel words; and the memory of his beloved Hero's image came over him, in the rare semblance that he loved it first; and the prince asking him if what he heard did not run like iron through his soul, he answered, that he felt as if he had taken poison while Borachio was speaking.

And the repentant Claudio implored forgiveness of the old man Leonato for the injury he had done his child, and promised, that whatever penance[52] Leonato would lay upon him for his fault in believing the false accusation against his betrothed[53] wife, for her dear sake he would endure it.

The penance Leonato enjoined[54] him was, to marry the next morning a cousin of Hero's, who, he said, was now his heir, and in person very like Hero. Claudio, regarding the solemn promise he made to Leonato, said he would marry this unknown lady, even though she were an Ethiop.

But his heart was very sorrowful, and he passed that night in tears, and in remorseful[55] grief, at the tomb which Leonato had erected for Hero.

52 penance ['penəns] (n.) 贖罪的苦行；懲罰
53 betrothed [bɪ'trouðd] (a.) 已婚的
54 enjoin [ɪn'dʒɔɪn] (v.) 命令；囑咐
55 remorseful [rɪ'mɔːrsfəl] (a.) 極為後悔的

When the morning came, the prince accompanied Claudio to the church, where the good friar, and Leonato and his niece, were already assembled, to celebrate a second nuptial; and Leonato presented to Claudio his promised bride. And she wore a mask, that Claudio might not discover her face. And Claudio said to the lady in the mask, "Give me your hand, before this holy friar. I am your husband, if you will marry me."

"And when I lived I was your other wife," said this unknown lady; and, taking off her mask, she proved to be no niece (as was pretended), but Leonato's very daughter, the Lady Hero herself.

We may be sure that this proved a most agreeable surprise to Claudio, who thought her dead, so that he could scarcely for joy believe his eyes; and the prince, who was equally amazed at what he saw, exclaimed, "Is not this Hero, Hero that was dead?"

Leonato replied, "She died, my lord, but while her slander lived."

The friar promised them an explanation of this seeming miracle, after the ceremony was ended; and was proceeding to marry them, when he was interrupted by Benedick, who desired to be married at the same time to Beatrice.

Beatrice making some demur[56] to this match, and Benedick challenging her with her love for him, which he had learned from Hero, a pleasant explanation took place; and they found they had both been tricked into a belief of love, which had never existed, and had become lovers in truth by the power of a false jest.

But the affection, which a merry invention had cheated them into, was grown too powerful to be shaken by a serious explanation; and since Benedick proposed to marry, he was resolved to think nothing to the purpose that the world could say against it; and he merrily kept up the jest, and swore to Beatrice, that he took her but for pity, and because he heard she was dying of love for him; and Beatrice protested, that she yielded but upon great persuasion, and partly to save his life, for she heard he was in a consumption.

---

56 demur [dɪˈmɜːr] (n.) 反對；異議 (v.) 提出異議

So these two mad wits were reconciled, and made a match of it, after Claudio and Hero were married; and to complete the history, Don John, the contriver of the villainy, was taken in his flight and brought back to Messina; and a brave punishment it was to this gloomy, discontented man, to see the joy and feastings which, by the disappointment of his plots, took place in the palace in Messina.

《無事生非》名句選

Leonato I will be flesh and blood;
For there was never yet philosopher
That could endure the toothache patiently,
However they have writ the style of gods,
And made a pish at chance and sufferance.
(V, i, 34–38)

李歐拿多 我是個血肉之軀的凡人；
從來就沒有一個哲學家
能夠平心靜氣忍受牙痛，
儘管他們曾以神來之筆，
藐視人生的災難與痛苦。

（第五幕，第一景，34-38行）

The Tempest

暴風雨

《暴風雨》導讀

《暴風雨》（*The Tempest*）是《莎士比亞全集》初版第一對開本裡的第一齣喜劇。此劇完成於 1611 年，同年 11 月在白廳（White Hall）於詹姆士國王御前演出。1613 年，莎士比亞的劇團再度受命演出此劇，以慶祝國王的女兒伊麗莎白出閣。這個劇本載歌載舞，戲劇效果佳，極適合在婚宴上演出。

魔法的劇情

本故事內容發生在一座杳無人煙的小島，主要角色普洛斯精通魔法，整齣戲就是由他透過法力「自編自導」而成，其中有引人入勝的狂風暴雨、千奇百變的魔幻法術、飛舞的隱形精靈、怪異畸形的半人半獸，還有奇妙有趣的純情故事等。

《暴風雨》和《連環錯》（*The Comedy of Errors*）一樣，都是莎劇中罕見吻合三一律的劇本——故事的地點都發生在荒島上，所有的事情都發生在同一天，並獲得圓滿結局。

《暴風雨》一劇追溯到幕啟前十二年，原為米蘭公爵的普洛斯因鑽研法術，埋首書堆，荒於政務，把王國轉交給弟弟安東尼代管。沒想到安東尼執政一段時日後，就與那不勒斯王聯合起來篡奪爵位，然後棄普洛斯和與其年幼的女兒米蘭達於大海上。

THE RAISING OF THE STORM.

隨後父女兩人漂流至荒島，後來普洛斯盼到最佳時機，當年出賣他的弟弟和那不勒斯王，如今帶領一群隨行人員往荒島駛來。於是他掀起一場暴風雨，以便讓兩人後悔當年所犯的過錯，最後並完成了米蘭達的婚事。

奇幻島的主題

奇幻島在民間文學中並不是罕見的主題，但當時的新聞時事可能才是莎士比亞最重要的靈感來源。 1609 年初夏，英國維吉尼亞公司（Virginia Company）的一艘巨大艦隊滿載四百多人，準備由普利茅斯（Plymouth）啟航，前往殖民地維吉尼亞州的詹姆士鎮（Jamestown）。未料七月某日發生強烈颶風，沖散艦隊，所幸所有艦隊船艇都在八月安全抵達詹姆士鎮，除了失去音訊的「海洋冒險號」（Sea Adventure）。

大家都認為「海洋冒險號」船上的人員凶多吉少，恐怕全數罹難。然而，就在隔年的五月，竟有兩艘小艇載著全數存活的「海洋冒險號」人員，奇蹟似地抵達詹姆士鎮，令眾人驚嘆不已。原來，他們一行人遇到船難後，無意間登陸在維吉尼亞海岸旁的百慕達島（Bermuda），因而保住了性命。

這座島嶼是當時水手口中聲名狼藉的惡魔島（Isle of Devils），船隻莫不避之，直到「海洋冒險號」抵達後，才發現那裡是人間仙境，島上不但食宿無慮，也有豐富的木材可供搭建船艇。這則消息一經披露，引起轟動，水手們也紛紛寫下這段奇異旅程。其中莎翁所閱讀到的，可能是由船上祕書史崔奇（William Strachey）在 1610 年 7 月 15 日所寫的船難獲救紀實手稿。

《暴風雨》中的島嶼約位於今日的地中海，介於突尼斯和那不勒斯之間，除了海洋冒險號登陸百慕達的事件，劇中的荒島也有美洲新大陸的色彩。法國人文思想家蒙田（Michel de Montaigne, 1533–1592）寫過一篇文章，名為〈論蠻夷〉（*Of Cannibals*）（但 cannibal 一字當時並沒有「食人肉」之意），內容在於歌頌美洲印第安族群的生活。

蒙田認為他們與大自然融合，簡單純樸，沒有政治紛擾和貧富問題，生活悠閒、平等、自然，彷彿就像柏拉圖的理想國，是一種完美理想的境界。〈論蠻夷〉的英文版在 1603 年出版，莎士比亞應該也看過這篇文章，因為第一對開本中的人物表，莎士比亞將卡力班描述成一個「野蠻畸形的奴隸」，而卡力班的名字 Caliban 就是由 Cannibal 裡的兩個子音對調而來的。

「技藝」與「自然」

《暴風雨》最重要的一個主題，就是「技藝」（art）與「自然」（nature）的分別。普洛斯所擁有的魔法是一種技藝，具有改變自然的力量。他的法力無邊，結合魔法與威權，主宰所有人的生命及意志：包括女兒米蘭達、活潑精靈艾瑞爾、半人半獸的怪物卡力班，以及斐迪南和那不勒斯王一行人。「自然」（nature）在中古暨文藝復興時期的意思是「種類」（kind），故「人性」（human nature）暗指人性千種萬類。

人性有高貴的一面，例如忠心護主的剛則婁，也有卑劣的一面，例如篡位、陷害兄長的安東尼，於此，「保有自然本性」和「合乎道德」兩種目標就可能衝突。普洛斯藉由外力，讓船上一干人飽受重重的心理試煉，如焦慮、誘惑、悲慟、恐懼、懺悔等，使他們改邪歸正，自己也重拾了爵位。

一場驚天動地的暴風雨，最後成為重生與覺悟的序曲，終而一片和諧，諸如此類的轉折與結局，都是典型的莎士比亞風格。

「奴役」與「自由」

普洛斯對艾瑞爾和卡力班的控制，觸及了「奴役」與「自由」的問題。普洛斯最得力的助手就是艾瑞爾，但艾瑞爾是個精靈，不屬於人類，他來去自如、不受拘束。他之所以服侍普洛斯，是為了要報恩。艾瑞爾一角和《仲夏夜之夢》（*A Midsummer Night's Dream*）裡的精靈帕克相仿，但兩者的個性天差地別。

普洛斯恩威並重，以紀律和記憶控制住艾瑞爾。命運截然不同的卡力班，則是另一個受到奴役的代表，他是女巫辛蔻雷的兒子，比艾瑞爾接近人類，普洛斯有意教化他，卻徒勞無功。

米蘭達是卡力班的相反典型，她天性善良溫馴，讓斐迪南一見到她就誤以為她是女神。在米蘭達的眼中，初見的人事物莫不美好，當她見到那不勒斯王和安東尼一群人時，說道：

O brave new world, that has such people in it.
啊，美麗的新世界，裡頭有如此這般的人們！

十九世紀的赫胥黎（Aldous Leonard Huxley, 1894–1963）引用了《美麗新世界》（*Brave New World*）來做書名，這一個詞語從此也幾乎就人盡皆知了。

「馬格斯」魔法師

普洛斯掀起的暴風雨雖然威力驚人，但本意並不在傷人。儘管復仇者心懷深怨重恨，莎士比亞卻盡力不讓普洛斯表現出多年的舊仇，而且在普洛斯達成目的後，就讓他棄絕魔法，表現出自制力。莎士比亞時期的人稱偉大的魔法師為「馬格斯」，大眾很著迷馬格斯這種人物。這種人物的特質是博學多聞、克勤律己、耐心求藝，因為惟有如此，才足以召喚自然界與超自然界的神祕力量。

馬格斯不像鄉野荒郊的巫婆，以療傷治病為號召或做些小奸小惡之事，也不像汲汲營營於化物成金的煉金師。馬格斯的形象是身穿織有神祕象徵的長袍，具有哲思智慧，行善必有善報。

儘管如此，當時的人提到馬格斯時，心頭仍不免有所餘悸，因為當時名聲最好的馬格斯為約翰·迪伊（John Dee, 1527–1608），他是伊麗莎白一世的顧問。他後來從自己家中的藏書室（也是英格蘭最大的私人圖書館）出走，焚身而亡。

浪漫劇

後世的批評家一向把《暴風雨》視為「浪漫劇」,莎翁晚期的作品幾乎都是浪漫劇,年代更早的《冬天的故事》(*The Winter's Tale*)也是。《暴風雨》的故事情節呼應了若干浪漫劇中常見的主題,例如:

▪ 父親對女兒的控制或依戀	《奧賽羅》《李爾王》
▪ 叛君行為	《哈姆雷特》《馬克白》
▪ 由宮廷至荒野,再回返宮廷的過程	《仲夏夜之夢》《皆大歡喜》
▪ 藉由技術,特別是戲中戲來操控他人	《無事生非》《哈姆雷特》
▪ 天性與教養的區別	《冬天的故事》
▪ 魔法的魅力	《仲夏夜之夢》

《暴風雨》是莎翁獨自創作的最後一齣劇本,十九世紀以降,就不乏將普洛斯視為莎翁化身的揣測。持此觀點的人認為莎翁就是以本劇告別劇場,而普洛斯在劇終將「魔法書和魔杖深埋地底下」,彷彿是莎翁離開劇場的心聲。雖然反對意見認為,莎翁鮮少將自己與劇中人物混為一談,更何況普洛斯是一個遭人放逐、懷恨在心、控制欲強的巫師。不過,劇場天地和魔法幻覺一樣,終究是以真實世界為基礎,故仍有人將普洛斯的魔法視為莎士比亞的生花妙筆。

二十世紀後,學術界開始以「殖民主義」(普洛斯與卡力班的主僕關係)和「女性主義」的觀點(普洛斯與米蘭達的父女關係）來探討《暴風雨》。 1990 年代，英國導演彼得‧格林那威（Peter Greenaway）執導的電影《魔法師的寶典》（*Prospero's Books*），便是改編自《暴風雨》。電影由英國實力派演員約翰‧吉爾格爵士（Sir John Gielgud）擔任普洛斯一角，當時他已年過八旬，戲劇生涯超過一甲子，而且還是個資歷豐富、演技精湛的莎劇演員，由他來飾演普洛斯，使觀眾不得不聯想到吉爾格、普洛斯、莎士比亞三人是否在劇場的魔法圈內，也有著微妙的交集。有興趣的讀者不妨參考之。

《暴風雨》人物表

Prospero 　普洛斯　米蘭公爵

Miranda 　米蘭達　普洛斯之女

Ariel 　艾瑞爾　精靈

Caliban 　卡力班　普洛斯的僕人

Antonio 　安東尼　普洛斯的弟弟，篡權者

Ferdinand 　斐迪南　那不勒斯王子

Gonzalo 　剛則婁　國王的臣子，曾幫助
　　　　　　　　　普洛斯

Sycorax 　辛蔻雷　女巫

The Tempest

There was a certain island in the sea, the only inhabitants of which were an old man, whose name was Prospero, and his daughter Miranda, a very beautiful young lady. She came to this island so young, that she had no memory of having seen any other human face than her father's.

They lived in a cave or cell, made out of a rock; it was divided into several apartments, one of which Prospero called his study; there he kept his books, which chiefly treated of magic, a study at that time much affected by all learned men: and the knowledge of this art he found very useful to him; for being thrown by a strange chance upon this island, which had been enchanted[1] by a witch called Sycorax, who died there a short time before his arrival, Prospero, by virtue of his art, released many good spirits that Sycorax had imprisoned in the bodies of large trees, because they had refused to execute her wicked commands. These

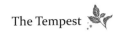

gentle spirits were ever after obedient to the will of Prospero. Of these Ariel was the chief.

The lively little sprite Ariel had nothing mischievous in his nature, except that he took rather too much pleasure in tormenting an ugly monster called Caliban, for he owed him a grudge[2] because he was the son of his old enemy Sycorax.

This Caliban, Prospero found in the woods, a strange misshapen thing, far less human in form than an ape: he took him home to his cell, and taught him to speak; and Prospero would have been very kind to him, but the bad nature which Caliban inherited[3] from his mother, Sycorax, would not let him learn anything good or useful: therefore he was employed like a slave, to fetch wood and do the most laborious offices; and Ariel had the charge of compelling[4] him to these services.

1 enchant [ɪnˈtʃænt] (v.) 施魔法
2 grudge [grʌdʒ] (n.) 怨恨；嫌隙
3 inherit [ɪnˈherɪt] (v.) 繼承；得自遺傳
4 compel [kəmˈpel] (v.) 強迫

When Caliban was lazy and neglected his work, Ariel (who was invisible to all eyes but Prospero's) would come slily and pinch[5] him, and sometimes tumble[6] him down in the mire[7]; and then Ariel, in the likeness of an ape, would make mouths at him. Then swiftly changing his shape, in the likeness of a hedgehog[8], he would lie tumbling in Caliban's way, who feared the hedgehog's sharp quills[9] would prick his bare feet. With a variety of suchlike vexatious[10] tricks Ariel would often torment him, whenever Caliban neglected the work which Prospero commanded him to do.

Having these powerful spirits obedient to his will, Prospero could by their means command the winds, and the waves of the sea. By his orders they raised a violent storm, in the midst of which, and struggling with the wild sea-waves that every moment threatened to swallow it up, he showed his daughter a fine large ship, which he told her was full of living beings like themselves.

---

5 pinch [pɪntʃ] (v.) 捏;擰
6 tumble ['tʌmbəl] (v.) 使跌倒
7 mire [maɪr] (n.) 泥坑
8 hedgehog ['hedʒhɑːg] (n.) 刺蝟
9 quill [kwɪl] (n.) 豪豬堅硬的長刺
10 vexatious [vek'seɪʃəs] (a.) 令人煩惱的

78

"O my dear father," said she, "if by your art you have raised this dreadful storm, have pity on their sad distress. See! the vessel[11] will be dashed[12] to pieces. Poor souls! they will all perish[13]. If I had power, I would sink the sea beneath the earth, rather than the good ship should be destroyed, with all the precious souls within her."

"Be not so amazed, daughter Miranda," said Prospero; "there is no harm done. I have so ordered it, that no person in the ship shall receive any hurt. What I have done has been in care of you, my dear child. You are ignorant who you are, or where you came from, and you know no more of me, but that I am your father, and live in this poor cave. Can you remember a time before you came to this cell? I think you cannot, for you were not then three years of age."

"Certainly I can, sir," replied Miranda.

"By what?" asked Prospero; "by any other house or person? Tell me what you can remember, my child."

---

11 vessel ['vesəl] (n.) 船；船艦
12 dash [dæʃ] (v.) 猛撞；撞擊
13 perish ['perɪʃ] (v.) 毀滅；死亡

79

Miranda said: "It seems to me like the recollection[14] of a dream. But had I not once four or five women who attended upon me?"

Prospero answered: "You had, and more. How is it that this still lives in your mind? Do you remember how you came here?"

"No, sir," said Miranda, "I remember nothing more."

"Twelve years ago, Miranda," continued Prospero, "I was Duke of Milan, and you were a princess, and my only heir[15]. I had a younger brother, whose name was Antonio, to whom I trusted everything; and as I was fond of retirement and deep study, I commonly left the management of my state affairs to your uncle, my false brother (for so indeed he proved). I, neglecting all worldly ends, buried among my books, did dedicate my whole time to the bettering of my mind. My brother Antonio being thus in possession of my power, began to think himself the duke indeed. The opportunity I gave him of making himself popular among my subjects awakened in his bad nature a proud ambition to deprive[16] me of my dukedom: this he soon effected with the aid of the King of Naples, a powerful prince, who was my enemy."

"Wherefore," said Miranda, "did they not that hour destroy us?"

---

14 recollection [ˌrekəˈlekʃən] (n.) 記憶
15 heir [er] (n.) 繼承人
16 deprive [dɪˈpraɪv] (v.) 剝奪；使喪失

"My child," answered her father, "they durst[17] not, so dear was the love that my people bore me. Antonio carried us on board a ship, and when we were some leagues[18] out at sea, he forced us into a small boat, without either tackle[19], sail, or mast[20]: there he left us, as he thought, to perish. But a kind lord of my court, one Gonzalo, who loved me, had privately placed in the boat, water, provisions[21], apparel, and some books which I prize above my dukedom."

"O my father," said Miranda, "what a trouble must I have been to you then!"

"No, my love," said Prospero, "you were a little cherub[22] that did preserve me. Your innocent smiles made me bear up against my misfortunes. Our food lasted till we landed on this desert island, since when my chief delight has been in teaching you, Miranda, and well have you profited by my instructions."

"Heaven thank you, my dear father," said Miranda. "Now pray tell me, sir, your reason for raising this sea-storm?"

"Know then," said her father, "that by means of this storm, my enemies, the King of Naples, and my cruel brother, are cast ashore upon this island."

17　durst [dɜːrst] (v.) 〔古〕dare 的過去式
18　league [liːg] (n.) 〔古〕里格（古老的長度單位，
　　海上距離的一里格，約 5.556 公里）
19　tackle ['tækəl] (n.) （用來操縱船帆或吊起重物等的）滑車
20　mast [mæst] (n.) 船桅
21　provisions [prə'vɪʒənz] (n.) 〔作複數形〕食物；食物供應
22　cherub ['tʃerəb] (n.) 天真無邪的可愛孩童

Having so said, Prospero gently touched his daughter with his magic wand, and she fell fast asleep; for the spirit Ariel just then presented himself before his master, to give an account of the tempest, and how he had disposed[23] of the ship's company, and though the spirits were always invisible to Miranda, Prospero did not choose she should hear him holding converse (as would seem to her) with the empty air.

"Well, my brave spirit," said Prospero to Ariel, "how have you performed your task?"

Ariel gave a lively description of the storm, and of the terrors of the mariners, and how the king's son, Ferdinand, was the first who leaped into the sea; and his father thought he saw his dear son swallowed up by the waves and lost.

"But he is safe," said Ariel, "in a corner of the isle, sitting with his arms folded, sadly lamenting[24] the loss of the king, his father, whom he concludes drowned. Not a hair of his head is injured, and his princely garments, though drenched in the sea-waves, look fresher than before."

"That's my delicate Ariel," said Prospero. "Bring him hither: my daughter must see this young prince. Where is the king, and my brother?"

"I left them," answered Ariel, "searching for Ferdinand, whom they have little hopes of finding, thinking they saw him perish. Of the ship's crew not one is missing; though each one thinks himself the only one saved; and the ship, though invisible to them, is safe in the harbor."

---

23 dispose [dɪˈspoʊz] (v.) 處理；處置
24 lament [ləˈment] (v.) 悲傷；惋惜

82

"Ariel," said Prospero, "thy charge is faithfully performed: but there is more work yet."

"Is there more work?" said Ariel. "Let me remind you, master, you have promised me my liberty. I pray, remember, I have done you worthy service, told you no lies, made no mistakes, served you without grudge or grumbling[25]."

"How now!" said Prospero. "You do not recollect what a torment I freed you from. Have you forgot the wicked witch Sycorax, who with age and envy was almost bent double? Where was she born? Speak; tell me."

"Sir, in Algiers," said Ariel.

"O was she so?" said Prospero. "I must recount[26] what you have been, which I find you do not remember. This bad witch, Sycorax, for her witchcrafts, too terrible to enter human hearing, was banished[27] from Algiers, and here left by the sailors; and because you were a spirit too delicate to execute her wicked commands, she shut you up in a tree, where I found you howling[28]. This torment, remember, I did free you from."

25 grumble ['grʌmbəl] (v.) 抱怨；牢騷

26 recount [rɪ'kaunt] (v.) 講述

27 banish ['bænɪʃ] (v.) 放逐；驅逐出境

28 howl [haʊl] (v.) 哀嚎

83

"Pardon me, dear master," said Ariel, ashamed to seem ungrateful; "I will obey your commands."

"Do so," said Prospero, "and I will set you free." He then gave orders what further he would have him do; and away went Ariel, first to where he had left Ferdinand, and found him still sitting on the grass in the same melancholy posture.

"O my young gentleman," said Ariel, when he saw him, "I will soon move you. You must be brought, I find, for the Lady Miranda to have a sight of your pretty person. Come. sir, follow me." He then began singing:

> *"Full fathom[29] five thy father lies:*
> *Of his bones are coral made;*
> *Those are pearls that were his eyes:*
> *Nothing of him that doth fade,*
> *But doth suffer a sea-change*
> *Into something rich and strange.*
> *Sea-nymphs[30] hourly ring his knell[31]:*
> *Hark! now I hear them—Ding-dong, bell."*

29 fathom [ˈfæðəm] (n.) 噚（測水深的單位，一噚是 1.829 公尺）

30 sea-nymph [ˈsiːnɪmf] (n.) 海仙子；海中女妖

31 knell [nel] (n.) 鐘聲；喪鐘聲

This strange news of his lost father soon roused the prince from the stupid fit into which he had fallen. He followed in amazement the sound of Ariel's voice, till it led him to Prospero and Miranda, who were sitting under the shade of a large tree. Now Miranda had never seen a man before, except her own father.

"Miranda," said Prospero, "tell me what you are looking at yonder[32]."

"O father," said Miranda, in a strange surprise, "surely that is a spirit. Lord! how it looks about! Believe me, sir, it is a beautiful creature. Is it not a spirit?"

"No, girl," answered her father; "it eats, and sleeps, and has senses such as we have. This young man you see was in the ship. He is somewhat altered by grief, or you might call him a handsome person. He has lost his companions, and is wandering about to find them."

Miranda, who thought all men had grave faces and grey beards like her father, was delighted with the appearance of this beautiful young prince; and Ferdinand, seeing such a lovely lady in this desert place, and from the strange sounds he had heard, expecting nothing but wonders, thought he was upon an enchanted island, and that Miranda was the goddess of the place, and as such he began to address her.

32 yonder ['jɑːndər] (adv.) 〔文〕那邊的；遠處（而可見）的

She timidly answered, she was no goddess, but a simple maid, and was going to give him an account of herself, when Prospero interrupted her. He was well pleased to find they admired each other, for he plainly perceived they had (as we say) fallen in love at first sight: but to try Ferdinand's constancy[33], he resolved to throw some difficulties in their way: therefore, advancing forward, he addressed the prince with a stern[34] air, telling him, he came to the island as a spy, to take it from him who was the lord of it.

"Follow me," said he. "I will tie your neck and feet together. You shall drink sea-water; shellfish, withered roots, and husks[35] of acorns shall be your food."

"No," said Ferdinand, "I will resist such entertainment, till I see a more powerful enemy," and drew his sword; but Prospero, waving his magic wand, fixed him to the spot where he stood, so that he had no power to move.

Miranda hung upon her father, saying: "Why are you so ungentle? Have pity, sir; I will be his surety[36]. This is the second man I ever saw, and to me he seems a true one."

---

33 constancy ['kɑːnstənsi] (n.) 堅定不移；恆久不變
34 stern [stɜːrn] (a.) 嚴格的；嚴厲的
35 husk [hʌsk] (n.) 外殼
36 surety ['sʊrɪti] (n.) 保證人

"Silence," said the father: "one word more will make me chide[37] you, girl! What! an advocate for an impostor[38]! You think there are no more such fine men, having seen only him and Caliban. I tell you, foolish girl, most men as far excel this, as he does Caliban." This he said to prove his daughter's constancy; and she replied,

"My affections are most humble. I have no wish to see a goodlier man."

"Come on, young man," said Prospero to the Prince; "you have no power to disobey me."

"I have not indeed," answered Ferdinand; and not knowing that it was by magic he was deprived of all power of resistance, he was astonished to find himself so strangely compelled to follow Prospero: looking back on Miranda as long as he could see her, he said, as he went after Prospero into the cave, "My spirits are all bound up, as if I were in a dream; but this man's threats, and the weakness which I feel, would seem light to me if from my prison I might once a day behold this fair maid."

---

37 chide [tʃaɪd] (v.) 〔文〕責罵；斥責
38 impostor [ɪmˈpɑːstər] (n.) 冒充者；騙子

87

Prospero kept Ferdinand not long confined[39] within the cell: he soon brought out his prisoner, and set him a severe task to perform, taking care to let his daughter know the hard labor he had imposed[40] on him, and then pretending to go into his study, he secretly watched them both.

Prospero had commanded Ferdinand to pile up some heavy logs of wood. Kings' sons not being much used to laborious work, Miranda soon after found her lover almost dying with fatigue.

"Alas!" said she, "do not work so hard; my father is at his studies, he is safe for these three hours; pray rest yourself."

"O my dear lady," said Ferdinand, "I dare not. I must finish my task before I take my rest."

"If you will sit down," said Miranda, "I will carry your logs the while."

But this Ferdinand would by no means agree to. Instead of a help Miranda became a hindrance[41], for they began a long conversation, so that the business of log-carrying went on very slowly.

THE PRINCE IN SERVITUDE.

39 confine [kənˈfaɪn] (v.) 關起來
40 impose [ɪmˈpoʊz] (v.) 加（負擔等）於；強加於
41 hindrance [ˈhɪndrəns] (n.) 妨礙的人或物

88

Prospero, who had enjoined Ferdinand this task merely as a trial of his love, was not at his books, as his daughter supposed, but was standing by them invisible, to overhear what they said.

Ferdinand inquired her name, which she told, saying it was against her father's express command she did so.

Prospero only smiled at this first instance of his daughter's disobedience, for having by his magic art caused his daughter to fall in love so suddenly, he was not angry that she showed her love by forgetting to obey his commands. And he listened well pleased to a long speech of Ferdinand's, in which he professed to love her above all the ladies he ever saw.

In answer to his praises of her beauty, which he said exceeded all the women in the world, she replied, "I do not remember the face of any woman, nor have I seen any more men than you, my good friend, and my dear father. How features are abroad, I know not; but, believe me, sir, I would not wish any companion in the world but you, nor can my imagination form any shape but yours that I could like. But, sir, I fear I talk to you too freely, and my father's precepts [42] I forget."

42 precept ['priːsept] (n.)（尤指行為的）規範；教訓

At this Prospero smiled, and nodded his head, as much as to say, "This goes on exactly as I could wish; my girl will be Queen of Naples."

And then Ferdinand, in another fine long speech (for young princes speak in courtly phrases), told the innocent Miranda he was heir to the crown of Naples, and that she should be his queen.

"Ah! sir," said she, "I am a fool to weep at what I am glad of. I will answer you in plain and holy innocence. I am your wife if you will marry me."

Prospero prevented Ferdinand's thanks by appearing visible before them.

"Fear nothing, my child," said he; "I have overheard, and approve of all you have said. And, Ferdinand, if I have too severely used you, I will make you rich amends[43], by giving you my daughter. All your vexations were but trials of your love, and you have nobly stood the test. Then as my gift, which your true love has worthily purchased, take my daughter, and do not smile that I boast she is above all praise."

He then, telling them that he had business which required his presence, desired they would sit down and talk together till he returned; and this command Miranda seemed not at all disposed to disobey.

When Prospero left them, he called his spirit Ariel, who quickly appeared before him, eager to relate what he had done with Prospero's brother and the King of Naples.

Ariel said he had left them almost out of their senses with fear, at the strange things he had caused them to see and hear. When fatigued with wandering about, and famished[44] for want of food, he had suddenly set before them a delicious banquet, and then, just as they were going to eat, he appeared visible before them in the shape of a harpy[45], a voracious[46] monster with wings, and the feast vanished away.

---

43 amends [ə'mendz] (n.) 〔作複數形〕賠罪；賠償
44 famish ['fæmɪʃ] (v.) 挨餓
45 harpy ['hɑːrpi] (n.) 〔希臘神話〕有女性面孔、長有鳥翅和爪子的殘暴怪物
46 voracious [vɔː'reɪʃəs] (a.) 狼吞虎嚥的；貪婪的

THE FAIRY BANQUET.

47 afflict [əˈflɪkt] (v.) 使痛苦；折磨

48 penitence [ˈpenɪtəns] (n.) 懺悔；贖罪

49 dainty [ˈdeɪnti] (a.) 美麗的；優雅的

90 Then, to their utter amazement, this seeming harpy spoke to them, reminding them of their cruelty in driving Prospero from his dukedom, and leaving him and his infant daughter to perish in the sea; saying, that for this cause these terrors were suffered to afflict[47] them.

The King of Naples, and Antonio the false brother, repented the injustice they had done to Prospero, and Ariel told his master he was certain their penitence[48] was sincere, and that he, though a spirit, could not but pity them.

"Then bring them hither, Ariel," said Prospero: "if you, who are but a spirit, feel for their distress, shall not I, who am a human being like themselves, have compassion on them? Bring them, quickly, my dainty[49] Ariel."

Ariel soon returned with the king, Antonio, and old Gonzalo in their train, who had followed him, wondering at the wild music he played in the air to draw them on to his master's presence. This Gonzalo was the same who had so kindly provided Prospero formerly with books and provisions, when his wicked brother left him, as he thought, to perish in an open boat in the sea.

Grief and terror had so stupefied[50] their senses, that they did not know Prospero. He first discovered himself to the good old Gonzalo, calling him the preserver of his life; and then his brother and the king knew that he was the injured Prospero.

Antonio, with tears and sad words of sorrow and true repentance, implored[51] his brother's forgiveness, and the king expressed his sincere remorse[52] for having assisted Antonio to depose[53] his brother: and Prospero forgave them; and, upon their engaging to restore his dukedom, he said to the King of Naples, "I have a gift in store for you too;" and opening a door, showed him his son Ferdinand playing at chess with Miranda.

Nothing could exceed the joy of the father and the son at this unexpected meeting, for they each thought the other drowned in the storm.

"O wonder!" said Miranda, "what noble creatures there are! It must surely be a brave world that has such people in it."

THE LOST PRINCE.

50 stupefy [ˈstuːpɪfaɪ] (v.) 使驚呆
51 implore [ɪmˈplɔːr] (v.) 懇求
52 remorse [rɪˈmɔːrs] (n.) 懊悔；自責
53 depose [dɪˈpouz] (v.) 迫使下台

The King of Naples was almost as much astonished at the beauty and excellent graces of the young Miranda, as his son had been. "Who is this maid?" said he; "she seems the goddess that has parted us, and brought us thus together."

"No, sir," answered Ferdinand, smiling to find his father had fallen into the same mistake that he had done when he first saw Miranda, "she is a mortal, but by immortal Providence[54] she is mine; I chose her when I could not ask you, my father, for your consent[55], not thinking you were alive. She is the daughter to this Prospero, who is the famous Duke of Milan, of whose renown I have heard so much, but never saw him till now: of him I have received a new life: he has made himself to me a second father, giving me this dear lady."

"Then I must be her father," said the king; "but oh! how oddly will it sound, that I must ask my child forgiveness."

"No more of that," said Prospero: "let us not remember our troubles past, since they so happily have ended."

54 Providence ['prɑːvɪdəns] (n.) 〔作大寫〕上帝；老天爺
55 consent [kən'sent] (n.) (v.) 同意；答應

And then Prospero embraced his brother, and again assured him of his forgiveness; and said that a wise overruling Providence had permitted that he should be driven from his poor dukedom of Milan, that his daughter might inherit the crown of Naples, for that by their meeting in this desert island, it had happened that the king's son had loved Miranda.

These kind words which Prospero spoke, meaning to comfort his brother, so filled Antonio with shame and remorse, that he wept and was unable to speak; and the kind old Gonzalo wept to see this joyful reconciliation[56], and prayed for blessings on the young couple.

Prospero now told them that their ship was safe in the harbor, and the sailors all on board her, and that he and his daughter would accompany them home the next morning.

"In the meantime," says he, "partake[57] of such refreshments as my poor cave affords; and for your evening's entertainment I will relate the history of my life from my first landing in this desert island."

---

56 reconciliation [ˌrekənsɪliˈeɪʃən] (n.) 和解
57 partake [pɑːrˈteɪk] (v.) 分享；分擔

He then called for Caliban to prepare some food, and set the cave in order; and the company were astonished at the uncouth[58] form and savage appearance of this ugly monster, who (Prospero said) was the only attendant he had to wait upon him.

Before Prospero left the island, he dismissed Ariel from his service, to the great joy of that lively little spirit; who, though he had been a faithful servant to his master, was always longing to enjoy his free liberty, to wander uncontrolled in the air, like a wild bird, under green trees, among pleasant fruits, and sweet-smelling flowers.

"My quaint[59] Ariel," said Prospero to the little sprite[60] when he made him free, "I shall miss you; yet you shall have your freedom."

"Thank you, my dear master;" said Ariel; "but give me leave to attend your ship home with prosperous gales[61], before you bid farewell to the assistance of your faithful spirit; and then, master, when I am free, how merrily I shall live!"

58 uncouth [ʌnˈkuːθ] (a.) 粗魯的;沒教養的
59 quaint [kweɪnt] (a.) 古怪的
60 sprite [spraɪt] (n.) 精靈
61 gale [geɪl] (n.) 大風;強風

Here Ariel sung this pretty song:

> *"Where the bee sucks, there suck I;*
> *In a cowslip's*[62] *bell I lie:*
> *There I crouch*[63] *when owls do cry.*
> *On the bat's back I do fly*
> *After summer Merrily.*
> *Merrily, merrily shall I live now*
> *Under the blossom that hangs on the bough."*

Prospero then buried deep in the earth his magical books and wand, for he was resolved never more to make use of the magic art. And having thus overcome his enemies, and being reconciled to his brother and the King of Naples, nothing now remained to complete his happiness, but to revisit his native land, to take possession of his dukedom, and to witness the happy nuptials[64] of his daughter and Prince Ferdinand, which the king said should be instantly celebrated with great splendor on their return to Naples.

At which place, under the safe convoy[65] of the spirit Ariel, they, after a pleasant voyage, soon arrived.

AMONG THE FLOWERS.

62 cowslip [ˈkauˌslɪp] (n.) 野櫻草

63 crouch [krautʃ] (v.) 蹲伏

64 nuptials [ˈnʌpʃəlz] (n.) 婚禮

65 convoy [ˈkɑːnvɔɪ] (n.) 護送

《暴風雨》名句選

Caliban   You taught me language, and my profit on it
Is, I know how to curse.
(I, ii, 363-364)

卡力班   你教我語言，而我從中獲得的
就是，我學會怎麼詛咒。
（第一幕，第二景，363-364 行）

Antonio   What's past is prologue; what to come,
In yours and my discharge.
(II, I, 253-254)

安東尼   過去的只是引子，以後要來的
就是你和我的事了。
（第二幕，第一景，253-254 行）

Prospero   We are such stuff
            As dreams are made on; and our little life
            Is rounded with a sleep.
            (IV, i, 156–158)

普洛斯   我們就是
          夢幻的原料;我們短暫的一生,
          前後都環繞著酣睡。
          (第四幕,第一景,156-158 行)

Miranda   O wonder!
           How many goodly creatures are there here!
           How beauteous mankind is! O brave new world
           That has such people in't!
           (V, i, 181–184)

米蘭達   哦,神奇!
          外頭有多少善良的生物!
          人類真是美麗!哦,美麗新世界
          裡頭竟有這樣的人兒!
          (第五幕,第一景,181-184 行)

羅密歐與茱麗葉

P. 26 富裕的柯譜雷家族和孟鐵古家族，是維洛那城的兩大望族。這兩個家族曾起齟齬，後來愈演愈烈，結下深仇大恨，最後連兩造的遠房親戚和部屬僕役都被牽連進去。孟家僕人只要碰見了柯家僕人，或是柯家人撞見了孟家人，就會互相叫罵，甚至發生喋血事件。這種一見面就吵架的事情時而可見，破壞了維洛那城街道的恬適清靜。

柯老爺舉辦一場盛宴，廣邀名媛貴客，維洛那城出名的美人都來了。只要不是孟家的人，誰來了都會受到歡迎。

P. 28 孟家的少爺羅密歐傾心的羅瑟琳也來參加柯家宴會。宴會上要是出現孟家的人，想必會出亂子，不過好友班弗禮還是說服了羅密歐少爺戴上面具，潛進宴會，去看他的羅瑟琳。讓羅密歐見識維洛那城那些出色的眾美人，再跟羅瑟琳比一比，（班弗禮說）羅密歐就會覺得他心目中的天鵝不過是隻烏鴉罷了。

羅密歐對班弗禮的話不以為然，不過因為他很喜歡羅瑟琳，所以他還是被說動了去參加宴會。羅密歐是個真摯熱情的人，他為愛失眠，常常自己一個人獨處，想的念的都是羅瑟琳。可是羅瑟琳看不上他，連報以最基本的禮貌或好意都沒有。班弗禮想帶他見識各方姑娘和朋友，讓他不要對羅瑟琳這麼痴情。

P. 30　　年輕的羅密歐、班弗禮和友人馬庫修，他們戴上面具來到了柯家的宴會上。柯老爺歡迎他們，告訴他們說，只要是腳上沒長繭的姑娘，誰都會想和她們跳舞。這個老人的心情很好，他還說起自己年輕的時候也會戴上面具，這樣才可以在美人的耳邊輕聲細語地對她們說些故事。

他們跳起了舞，這時，舞池中一位美若天仙的姑娘，讓羅密歐看得目瞪口呆。羅密歐感到，因為有她的存在，火炬變得更加光輝。在這黑夜裡，她的美猶如黑人所戴上的珍貴寶石。「此美只應天上有，讓人不敢褻玩焉！」她站在眾女伴之間，（他說）就好像一隻白鴿站在烏鴉群裡，看起來是那麼閃閃動人、完美無瑕。

未料，羅密歐的喃喃讚美，被柯老爺的姪子提伯特給聽到了，提伯特認出了那是羅密歐的聲音。

P. 32　　這個提伯特的脾氣很火爆，（他是這樣說的）他不能容忍孟家人蒙面混進來嘲弄譏諷這個隆重場合。他破口大罵，非常氣憤，恨不得一拳打死這個年輕的羅密歐。

然而提伯特的伯父柯老爺不許他當場鬧事，一來是因為考慮到其他的客人，二來也是因為羅密歐向來是個正人君子，維洛那城的人們無不稱讚他是個品德很好、很有教養的年輕人。

提伯特只好按捺住脾氣，他發誓說，改天一定要這個擅自闖入的可惡孟家人付出慘痛的代價。

跳完舞之後，羅密歐望著那位姑娘所站的地方。有了面具的掩護，羅密歐敢情放肆些。他壯起膽子，溫柔地牽起她的手，說她的手好比是神殿，而他自己是一個羞赧的朝聖者；如果他這麼一碰，褻瀆了她的手，他願意親吻它，當做贖罪。

P. 33　　姑娘回答：「善心的朝聖者，你的朝拜也未免太隆重多禮了。聖徒的手，朝聖者只可以摸，不可以吻。」

「聖徒和朝聖者都有嘴唇吧？」羅密歐說。

姑娘說：「有，那是做禱告用的。」

P. 34　　羅密歐說：「哦，親愛的聖徒，那就請聽我的祈禱，應允我吧，不然我就會陷入絕望之地了。」

這些曖昧的對話還沒說完，姑娘的母親就把她給叫走了。羅密歐打聽她母親的身分後，得知這位讓他心動不已的絕色美人，就是年輕的茱麗葉——孟家大仇人柯老的女兒及繼承人。他這下明白了自己無意間愛上了仇家的人。

他很糾結，因為他放不掉這份感情。當茱麗葉知道和她說話的是孟家的羅密歐後，也同樣忐忑不安。她和羅密歐一樣，糊里糊塗地一下子就墜入情網。這份愛情來得令她錯愕，她愛上仇家的人，而那是她的家人要她痛恨的人。

P. 36　　羅密歐和友人待到了半夜才離開，之後他一溜煙不見人影，因為他的魂留在孟家了，走不開。他從茱麗葉屋後的果園圍牆翻進去，想著這位新歡。不久，樓上的窗口邊出現了茱麗葉。她看起來那麼美，猶如東方閃爍的陽光。在旭日的耀眼光輝下，羅密歐覺得照在果園裡的微弱月光，顯得憔悴又蒼白。

她托著香腮，羅密歐巴不得自己就是她手上的手套，可以撫摸她的臉頰。她以為周遭沒人，就嘆了一口長長的氣，唉了一聲：「哎呀！」

聽到茱麗葉的聲音，羅密歐非常興奮。他輕聲地說，輕到茱麗葉也沒能聽見：「耀眼的天使，再說些話吧。妳像天使般地出現在我的上方，像長著翅膀的信使從天而降，凡人都要抬頭仰望。」

P. 38　茱麗葉不察隔牆有耳，只想著今晚所邂逅的戀情。她呼喊著意中人的名字（她以為他不在場）：「哦，羅密歐！羅密歐！為什麼你要是羅密歐？為了我，你就不要認你的父親，換個姓吧。如果你不願意，那麼只要你發誓會永遠愛我，那我就不再當柯家的人。」

羅密歐受到這番話的鼓舞，滿心想回應她，但他也很想再聽她說下去。她熱情澎湃，繼續自言自語（她以為），說羅密歐不該是羅密歐，不該是孟家的人。但願他姓別的姓，要不然就把那個討厭的姓換掉，反正姓又不是長在身上的東西。只要把姓丟掉，他就可以得到她整個人了。

聽到這些深情款款的話，羅密歐再也按捺不住。他逕自接她的話，就好像她剛剛真的在對他講話一樣。他說，她要是不喜歡羅密歐這個名字，那他就不要叫羅密歐，她可以叫他「愛人」或任何什麼名字都可以，只要她喜歡就行。

P. 40 聽到花園裡有男人的聲音，茱麗葉嚇了一跳。起初，她不知道半夜裡躲在暗處偷聽祕密的人是誰，但是情人的耳朵就是特別尖，雖然沒聽過羅密歐說過幾句話，可是當他再開口時，她立刻就認出了是年輕的羅密歐。她警告他說，孟家的人爬過果園圍牆是很危險的，萬一被她家人發現，他就死定了。

羅密歐回答：「哎呀，妳的眼睛比他們的二十把劍都還更厲害。姑娘，只要妳給我一個溫柔的眼神，他們的仇恨就奈何不了我。要是不能擁有妳的愛，那我寧可死在他們的仇恨裡，也不願含恨活下去。」

「你是怎麼到這裡的？誰帶你來的？」茱麗葉問。

「是愛情帶我來的。我不會航海，但就算妳遠在天邊，為了妳，我也要冒險出海。」羅密歐回答。

P. 42 茱麗葉想起剛才不小心讓羅密歐知道了自己的心意，臉頰不禁一陣緋紅，還好是在黑夜裡，羅密歐不會看到。

她想收回她的話，但覆水難收。她也想謹守禮法，像個大家閨秀，和情人保持距離，然後蹙著眉頭，讓追求者碰個大釘子，裝出一副害羞或冷漠的樣子，卻迎還拒，這樣情人才不會覺得她們太容易就被追到手，畢竟，愈難得到的東西愈珍貴。

不過，她的情況容不得她又推又拒，玩玩以退為進的求偶把戲。她沒想到羅密歐會近在咫尺偷聽她的親口告白。

P.45　於是她就索性坦承他剛剛所聽到的都是真心話，還稱呼他是「英俊的孟鐵古」（愛情可以把刺耳的姓變得很甜蜜）。她請他不要因為她這麼快表達愛意，就以為她很輕浮隨便，一切只能怪（如果這樣有錯的話）今晚不湊巧，不小心吐露了心意。

她還說，用一般的婦道來看，她對他的舉止也許不夠端莊，但她比那些假裝矜持靦腆而造作的人都更為真心。

羅密歐準備對天發誓，發誓自己完全不認為這樣一位貞潔姑娘會有半點不名譽之處，但她要他不要發誓。她是很喜歡他，可是她並不喜歡當晚就發誓，那樣會顯得太輕率、魯莽又突兀。

P.46　但羅密歐急著當晚就和她互定情盟，而她說，在他還沒開口要求之前，她就已經給他了。這意思是指他已經聽過她的表白了。不過她想要收回那些話，重新享受對他起誓的喜悅，因為她有的是比大海還深、還浩蕩的愛。

兩人正情話綿綿時，茱麗葉被奶媽叫了進去。天都快亮了，和她同睡的奶媽覺得她該上床了。之後她又匆忙

跑出來，跟羅密歐說了三、四句話。她告訴他，要是他真心愛她、有意娶她，她明天就會派人去找他，選個黃道吉日和他結婚，她要把自己的命運交付給他，跟隨他到天涯海角。

他們在決定此事時，奶媽又叫她，她就跑進跑出，來來回回。她很捨不得讓羅密歐走，就像小女孩捨不得放小鳥走一樣，小鳥才從手上跳離一會兒，就趕緊用絲線把牠拉回來。羅密歐也同樣依依不捨，對情人來說，最美的音樂就是彼此在夜裡互相傾吐的話語。

P.48 最後他們終於道別，互祝對方有個好眠。他們分手時，東方已經泛白。羅密歐不想睡覺，他滿腦子都是情人和兩人幸福的邂逅。他沒回家，而是繞到附近的修道院去找勞倫斯修士。

這個好心修士已經起身禱告，看到年輕的羅密歐一大早就出門，就猜出他一定是因為什麼少年情懷而整夜失眠。

他是猜對了羅密歐為情一夜未眠，可是他猜錯對象了，以為他是為羅瑟琳而失眠。

　　但是當羅密歐說他剛愛上了茱麗葉，想請修士當天為他們證婚時，修士抬起雙眼、舉起雙手，對羅密歐的變心大為吃驚。修士私下明白羅密歐是如何地愛羅瑟琳，也知道他如何嘀咕她看不起他。修士於是說，年輕人不是用真心來愛，而是用眼睛來愛。

P. 50　　然而羅密歐回答，羅瑟琳並不愛他，修士不也常怪他不該對她太過痴情的嗎？而他和茱麗葉是兩情相悅。修士只好勉強接受他的理由，他心裡想，或許茱麗葉和羅密歐這對年輕人的親事，會是消除柯孟兩家多年仇恨的好方法。這位好心的修士和兩家都很要好，所以最為兩家之間的嫌隙感到惋惜。他常想調解兩家的糾紛，不過都沒有成功。他一方面因為有此打算，一方面也是因為他很疼愛年輕的羅密歐，無法拒絕他，老人家便同意為兩人主婚。

　　羅密歐頓時感到萬分幸福。依約派人去找羅密歐的茱麗葉知道了此事，就早早趕到了勞倫斯的修道密室，兩人就在那裡締結了神聖的婚姻。好心的修士祈禱上天能夠眷顧這椿姻緣，藉由這對孟柯兩家年輕人的結合，可以把兩家的舊仇宿怨都埋葬掉。

P. 53　　茱麗葉在婚禮結束後就趕忙回家，焦急地等待夜晚來臨，因為羅密歐說

晚上要來他們昨晚碰面的果園裡找她。這段時間對她來說真是難熬，她就像一個在盛大節日前夕感到焦躁的小孩，雖然得到了新衣服，卻要等到隔天早上才能穿。

當日約莫正午，羅密歐的友人班弗禮和馬庫修走在維洛那城的街道上時，碰上了一群柯家的人，而走在最前頭的正是火爆的提伯特。他就是那個在柯老爺的晚宴上，氣沖沖地想和羅密歐幹一架的提伯特。

提伯特一看到馬庫修，就粗魯地指責他和孟家的羅密歐往來。馬庫修和提伯特一樣脾氣暴戾、血氣方剛，他很衝地對他的指責回嘴。班弗禮竭力調解，想要平息兩人的怒氣，可是他們還是吵了起來。當羅密歐剛好經過時，凶悍的提伯特將矛頭從馬庫修轉向羅密歐，蔑稱他是惡棍。

P. 54　羅密歐極力想避免和提伯特發生衝突，因為他是茱麗葉的親戚，茱麗葉也很喜歡他。此外，這位年輕的孟家人生性就聰明溫和，從沒捲進過這種家族爭鬥。再加上「柯譜雷」是他心愛姑娘的姓，如今這個姓氏與其說是激怒人的口令，還不如說是消解仇恨的咒語。

他設法和提伯特講道理，客氣地以「好柯譜雷」來稱呼他，彷彿儘管他是孟家的人，他在喊出這個姓氏時，暗地裡也有些喜悅。無奈提伯特恨透

EITHER·THOV·OR·I·OR·BOTH
MVST·GO·WITH·HIM

所有孟家的人，他拔出劍，根本
不聽什麼道理。馬庫修不知道羅
密歐向提伯特求和的原因，他看
到他這樣吞忍，以為他怕事，想
委曲求全，所以他就口出惡語，
挑釁提伯特，繼續爭吵。他們兩
個人接著打了起來，羅密歐和班
弗禮努力想把兩個人分開，但是
都沒有成功。最後，馬庫修受到
了致命的攻擊，倒地不起。

P. 56　　馬庫修一死，羅密歐就再也
忍不住，他回敬提伯特，也蔑稱
他是惡棍。他們動起手來，最後，羅密歐殺死了提伯特。

　　這個可怕的亂子發生在日正當中的維洛那城中心。消息一
傳開，出事地點很快就圍來了大批的民眾，柯孟兩家的老爺和
夫人都來到了現場，親王隨即也趕了過來。親王和被提伯特殺
死的馬庫修是親戚，又加上他理政時常被孟柯兩家的事鬧得不
得安寧，所以他下決定心一定要揪出兇手，並且嚴加懲治。

P. 57　　班弗禮親眼目睹了這場打鬥，親王要他陳述事情的原委。
在不會不利於羅密歐的情況下，班弗禮盡可能據實以告，並盡
量為羅密歐辯解，以降低羅密歐在整個事件中的參與程度。

　　柯夫人失去了親人提伯特，十分悲痛，一心只想報復。她
請親王嚴懲兇手，不要聽信班弗禮的話，班弗禮是孟家的人，
是羅密歐的朋友，說話一定會有所偏袒。就這樣，她告了自己
的新女婿，雖然她還不曉得羅密歐就是自己的女婿、茱麗葉的
丈夫。

P. 58　　這一邊，孟家夫人則為孩子的性命求情。她辯說，羅密歐不應該為殺死提伯特而受罰，因為提伯特先殺了馬庫修，犯法在先。

　　親王慎查事實，不被兩個激動婦人的叫喊所動搖。他宣布判決，依判決，羅密歐將被放逐出維洛那城。

　　這對年輕的茱麗葉來說，實在是個難以承受的消息。她才當了幾個鐘頭的新娘子，如今一道命令下來就要永遠分離！消息傳來時，她一開始是生羅密歐的氣，怪他殺了親愛的堂哥。

　　她說他是俊美的暴君、天使般的魔鬼、烏鴉般黑的鴿子、狼心的羔羊、花朵的外表下藏著蛇蠍心腸，她說著這些自相矛盾的稱呼，透露出內心的愛恨掙扎。

P. 60　　最後，愛情佔了上風。她因羅密歐殺死堂哥而流的傷心淚，變成了慶幸的眼淚，因為提伯特想要殺她的丈夫，而她的丈夫還活著。但後來她又哭了起來，因為傷心羅密歐要被放逐。死了好幾個提伯特的消息，都還不及放逐這個字眼更教她驚駭。

　　在那場打鬥之後，羅密歐躲進了勞倫斯的修道密室。他在密室裡得知了親王的判決，他覺得這個判決比死刑還可怕。對他來說，出了維洛那城的牆外，就沒有別的世界了。要是見不到茱麗葉，那他就活不下去。有茱麗葉的地方就是天堂，否則就是煉獄、折磨、地獄。

　　好心的修士原本想安慰他說一切都是命中注定，莫過於悲傷，但這個發狂的年輕人什麼也聽不下去。他像瘋子似地扯自己的頭髮，整個人癱在地上，說要量量自己的墓穴大小。後來心愛的妻子派人捎信來，他才從這種不堪的情況中振作了些。修士趁機警告他，說他剛才的軟弱德性太沒有男子氣概了。

P. 61　　他殺了提伯特，難道也要把自己殺掉，把和他相依為命的心愛妻子殺掉嗎？修士說，人在表面上看起來很高貴，可是要是少了堅定的勇氣，那就不過是一尊蠟像罷了。他犯的是死罪，親王卻只親口宣判驅逐他，法律對他已經很寬容了。本來是提伯特想殺他的，結果卻是他殺了提伯特，這一點也很僥倖。茱麗葉還活著，而

且成為他的愛妻（誰也料想不到）。就這點來看，他是最幸福的人了。

　　修士跟他說，他是如何的幸福，但羅密歐就像個乖張無禮的丫頭，理都不理。修士請他當心，（他說）自暴自棄讓人不得善終。

P. 62　　待羅密歐平靜些，修士建議他，當晚就偷偷去和茱麗葉道別，然後馬上前往曼圖亞，在那裡落腳，直到修士找到機會宣布他們已經結婚的消息，這或許會是使兩家盡釋前嫌的好方法。修士自信到時一定能說動親王赦免羅密歐，雖然羅密歐現在離開得很痛苦，但到時候他就能懷著二十倍的喜悅返鄉。

　　修士的策略說服了羅密歐，他告別修士去找妻子，打算當晚待在她那裡，天一亮就獨自動身前往曼圖亞。好心的修士答應不時會捎信去曼圖亞給他，讓他知道家中的情況。

當晚，羅密歐從之前半夜偷聽到茱麗葉告白的果園裡潛入閨房，和心愛的妻子共度了一夜。這一夜充滿真摯的欣喜和痴迷，但一想到即將到來的分離，一想到白天所發生的不幸事情，這一晚的喜悅和與愛人相伴的幸福，又不幸地給沖淡了。

P. 65 不受歡迎的黎明似乎來得太快。茱麗葉聽到雲雀的晨鳴，她想騙自己相信那是夜鶯的夜啼。但唱歌的，的確是雲雀，那個聲音是那麼嘈雜難聽，而東方的曙光也無疑地指出該是戀人分手的時刻了。

羅密歐帶著沉重的心情告別愛妻，答應到了曼圖亞一定會常寫信回來給她。他從她房間的窗戶爬下來，站在地上抬頭望她。因為她心裡有著不祥預感，所以眼前這一幕他看起來像是墓穴裡的屍首。他對她也有同樣的感受，可是他得趕緊離開。如果他天亮後被發現還待在維洛那城內，那他就得被處死。

P. 66 對這對不幸的戀人來說，悲劇才剛要開始。羅密歐走後沒有幾天，柯老爺向茱麗葉談起一門婚事。他作夢也沒想到女兒已經結婚了，他為她所挑選的丈夫是年少英勇的高貴紳士裴力司伯爵。如果年輕的茱麗葉沒有遇到羅密歐，那他倒還配得上她。

父親所提的親事讓擔驚受怕的茱麗葉非常茫然。她說，自己還太年輕，不適合結婚，提伯特又剛死不久，她提不起精

262

神，無法高高興興地面對丈夫，況且柯家才剛辦完喪事，如果接著就舉行婚宴，會顯得很不成體統。她用各種理由來推卻婚事，就是不提真正的原因：她已經嫁作人婦。

但柯老爺不理會她的理由，專橫地要她做好準備，在下週四就要嫁給裴力司。他為她找的丈夫年輕有錢又高貴，即使是維洛那城最高傲的姑娘，也會歡歡喜喜地接受這門親事。也因此，當他看到茱麗葉拒絕時，就以為她只是在故作姿態。他不容許她阻礙自己的大好前程。

P. 68　　茱麗葉無路可走，便跑去請教好心的修士。她有苦惱時，一向都會找修士談。修士問她是否能下決心採取孤注一擲的方法，她回答，她心愛的丈夫還活著，如果要她嫁給裴力司，那她寧可活著躺進墳墓裡。修士叫她先回家，裝出一副開心的樣子，並依父親的意思，答應嫁給裴力司。修士給她一小瓶藥水，要她在明天晚上，也就是婚禮的前一天晚上，把藥水喝下去。藥水喝下去之後的四十二小時之內，她會全身冰冷，就像死屍一樣。這樣，

新郎隔天早上來迎娶她時，就會以為她已經斷氣。接著，依照地方習俗，她會被抬上棺，然後不蓋上棺蓋地運到族墳裡去下葬。修士說，要是她能克服女人家的膽怯，同意這個可怕的考驗，那麼吞下藥水四十二個小時之後，她必定醒來（確定效力會如此），這一切都只會像是一場夢而已。而在她醒來之前，

他會通知她的丈夫這件事，要她丈夫在夜裡趕來，把她帶去曼圖亞。

P. 71 　　愛情和嫁給裴力司的恐懼，讓年輕的茱麗葉有了力量去做這件可怕的事。她接過修士的藥水，答應照他的指示去做。

　　她在從修道院回來的途中，碰見了年輕的裴力司伯爵，她得體地假裝答應做他的新娘子。這對柯老爺和柯夫人來說，真是個好消息，老人家們頓時又顯得喜氣洋洋。她之前拒絕伯爵的親事，柯老爺很不高興，現在聽到她願意乖乖聽話，就又寵愛起她了。

　　全家上上下下趕忙張羅即將到來的婚禮，為了準備一場維洛那城空前的盛大喜宴，柯家多少錢都捨得花。

　　週三晚上，茱麗葉把藥喝下去。她心中有許多顧慮，擔心修士會因為要逃避為她和羅密歐證婚的責任，所以拿毒藥給她吃，不過人人都知道修士是一個聖潔的人。

P. 72 　　她又擔心，要是她醒過來時，還不見羅密歐來，那可怕的墓穴會不會把她嚇得精神錯亂？那裡躺著的都是柯家人的屍骨，而且還躺著渾身是血、在壽衣裡逐漸腐爛的提伯特，她想起了以前聽過的那些靈魂留連屍處的故事。接著她又想起對羅密歐的愛和對裴力司的嫌惡，才不顧一切地把藥水一口吞下去，隨後失去了知覺。

　　一早，年輕的裴力司帶著樂隊前來喚醒新娘，但他沒有看到活生生的茱麗葉，只看到房間裡一片死寂，躺著一具死屍。

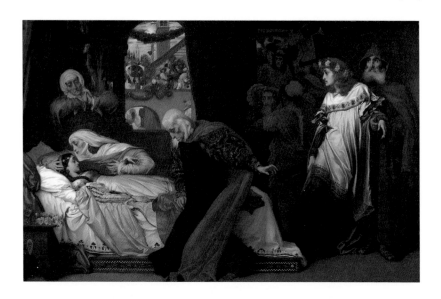

　　裴力司的期待如此落空！整個屋子裡一片混亂！可憐的裴力司為他的新娘子痛哭，可恨的死神把他的新娘子拐走，在他們還沒成親之前就拆散他們。

　　柯老爺夫人的哀號更是令人不忍聽聞，他們膝下就只有這個孩子，就只有這麼一個可愛的可憐孩子，可以帶給他們快樂和安慰。在這兩位設想周到的父母眼見這一門親事即將要送她飛上枝頭時（他們以為），無情的死神卻從他們眼前把她給帶走。

　　現在，為婚禮所預備好的一切，變成哀戚喪事之用。婚禮喜宴變成喪禮筵席，婚禮的詩歌改成悲傷的輓歌，輕快的樂器換成沉鬱的喪鐘，要用來撒在新娘走道上的鮮花，如今用來撒在屍體上。不需要牧師為她證婚，而是需要牧師為她主持葬禮。她是被帶進教堂，但這並沒有為活著的人增添愉快的希望，而是不幸地又多了一位死者。

P. 75　　勞倫斯修士派人去通知羅密歐這是一場假葬禮，他的愛妻只是表面上詐死，暫時躺在墳墓裡，等著他去陰森的巨室裡把她救出來。但壞消息總是傳得比好消息快，修士派去的人都還沒趕到達曼圖亞，茱麗葉的死亡噩耗就傳到羅密歐的耳裡了。

在這之前，羅密歐還一直很雀躍快活。他夜裡夢見自己死了（這夢真奇怪，死了的人還能思考），妻子來找他，她看到他死了就親吻他，把氣吹進他的唇間，結果他竟然復活，而且還當上了皇帝！

P. 76 這時有人從維洛那城送信來，他想一定會如夢兆所示，送來什麼好消息。然而，消息卻偏偏和他的美夢相反，真正死掉的是妻子，而且他再怎麼親吻她，她也不會復活了。他立刻叫人備馬，決定當晚回維洛那城，去妻子的墳墓裡看她。

人在絕望之際，很容易產生不好的念頭。他想起曼圖亞有個窮藥師，他日前才打從他的店門口經過。藥師的外表看起來像要飯的，一副餓相，店裡的骯髒架子上所放的空罐子等各種東西，都讓他看起來很寒愴潦倒。他當時說（也許有些擔心他的悲慘生活，到頭來會落入無可挽回的結局）：

「依曼圖亞的法律，賣毒藥是死罪，可是如果有人需要，這裡有個可憐蟲可以賣給他。」

P. 78 羅密歐想起他的這句話，便前去找他。藥師假裝有所遲疑，但等羅密歐掏出錢後，貧窮就不容他抵抗了。他把毒藥賣給羅密歐，告訴他只要他把毒藥吞下，哪怕他擁有二十個男人的氣力，照樣馬上斃命。

羅密歐帶上毒藥朝著維洛那城前進，準備去愛妻的墳墓裡見妻子。換句話說，等他把妻子看個夠了以後，他就要吞下毒藥，和妻子葬在一塊。

他在半夜時抵達維洛那城。他找到教堂墓園，墓園的正中央就是柯家的族墳。他拿出燭火、鏟子和鐵鍬，就在他正要撬開墓門時，一個聲音打斷了他。這個聲音稱他是「可惡的孟鐵古」，要他住手，不要做不法之事。

P. 79　　這個人是年輕的裴力司伯爵。在半夜這個不當的時刻裡，他來茱麗葉的墳上獻花、哭泣，而她本來應該已經是他的新娘子了。他不知道羅密歐對死者有什麼企圖，只曉得他是孟家的人，（他以為）是所有柯家人的死敵。他以為羅密歐三更半夜跑來，一定是想要侮辱死者的屍體，所以就很生氣地叫他住手。況且羅密歐還是個罪犯，依照維洛那城的法律，只要他在城裡被逮到，就是死罪，裴力司因此要逮捕他。

　　羅密歐要裴力司走開，否則下場就會和葬在這個墳墓裡的提伯特一樣。他警告裴力司不要惹他，逼他殺他，在他身上再幹一票。

　　但伯爵不屑他的警告，只當他是重犯，動手要抓他，兩人於是打了起來。最後，裴力司倒地不起。

P. 80　　羅密歐走近裴力司，用火把的光一看，才知道他殺的人正是要娶茱麗葉的人（他由曼圖亞回來的途中知道了這件事）。厄運彷彿讓羅密歐和裴力司作了伴，羅密歐拉起這個斷氣年輕人的手，說要把他葬在勝利的墳墓裡，也就是茱麗葉的墳墓。

　　羅密歐打開墳墓，墳裡躺著他的妻子。妻子仍舊美麗無比，看來，死神一點也沒辦法讓她的容貌或膚色變樣。或者

說，瘦巴巴、令人厭惡的死神怪物也愛上了她，所以把她留在
墓裡讓自己高興。她躺在那裡，依舊那麼嬌嫩明艷，她的樣子
就跟她剛吞下麻醉藥後睡去一樣。她的旁邊躺著身穿沾滿血漬
壽衣的提伯特，羅密歐一看到提伯特的屍體，就對著屍體請求
原諒。因為茱麗葉的緣故，他稱提伯特為「堂哥」，還說要幫
他個忙：殺掉他的仇人。

P. 81　　在此，羅密歐親吻妻子的雙唇以做為訣別。他吞下藥師賣
給他的毒藥，好把疲憊身上的厄運重擔給擺脫掉。和茱麗葉服
下的假毒藥不一樣，羅密歐的毒藥會叫人送命。茱麗葉的藥逐
漸失去藥效，她即將甦醒過來，然後抱怨羅密歐不守時——或
是說他來得太早了。

P. 82　　此時已經到了修士保證她會醒過來的時間了。修士剛得
知，因為一些事不湊巧，他派去曼圖亞的信差在路上給耽擱
了，始終未能把信送到羅密歐的手裡。修士於是帶著尖鋤和燈
籠趕來，準備把關在墳裡的茱麗葉救出來。當他看到柯家墓裡
透出燈火時，他吃了一驚。隨後，他看到附近有劍和血跡，雙
雙斷氣的羅密歐和裴力司則躺在墓旁。

　　在他還來不及思考和推測這些不幸的事情是如何發生時，
茱麗葉在昏迷中甦醒了過來。她看到一旁的修士後，才想起自
己怎麼會來到這個地方。她問起羅密歐，但修士聽到一陣噪
音，就叫她不要再繼續這種非自然的睡眠，趕緊離開這個死者
之地，因為擋不住的力量就要來阻礙他們的計畫了。修士聽到
有人走近，便落荒而逃。

P. 84　　茱麗葉看到她心愛的情人手裡握著杯子，猜他是服毒而
亡。要是杯中還留有殘藥，她一定也會把它吞下去。她吻著
他那還有餘溫的雙唇，想嚐他唇上所可能殘留的毒藥。隨後，

　　她聽到眾人走近的聲音，便迅速拔出自己隨身佩帶的短劍，然後往自己身上刺下去，倒在忠誠的羅密歐身邊。

P. 85　　這時趕來了守衛。裴力司伯爵的僮僕看到主人和羅密歐在打鬥，就急忙跑去找人來幫忙。城民們在維洛那城的街道上奔相走告，因為聽到的傳言片斷不全，所以有人嚷著「裴力司！」，有人喊著「羅密歐！」，有人叫著「茱麗葉！」，一片混亂。隨後，孟老爺和柯老爺也被這場騷動吵醒，跟著親王一起前來探個究竟。

　　一些守衛們抓到了修士。修士從教堂墓園那邊走過來，他打著哆嗦、嘆著氣，還流著眼淚，令人起疑。大批人群圍聚在柯家族墓旁，對於這件離奇的慘劇，親王要修士把他知道的事都說出來。

P. 86 　　修士當著孟老爺和柯老爺的面，詳實述說兩個孩子之間的生死戀，並表示自己促成了他們的婚事，目的是希望兩人的婚姻可以結束兩家長久以來的爭執。他說，躺在那裡的羅密歐是茱麗葉的丈夫，躺在那裡的茱麗葉是羅密歐忠貞的妻子。他還沒找適當機會宣布兩人的婚姻時，就有人來向茱麗葉提親。為了避免犯重婚罪，茱麗葉就（依他的建議）吞下安眠藥詐死。這期間，他寫信給羅密歐，要他在藥效消退的時候把茱麗葉帶走，但信差不幸誤事，羅密歐始終沒有收到信。

　　接下來發生的事情修士就不知道了，只知道自己來這裡要把茱麗葉從墓穴裡救出去，卻看到裴力司伯爵和羅密歐都已經斷氣。

P. 87 　　看到裴力司和羅密歐在打鬥的僮僕，以及和羅密歐一同從維洛那城前來的僕人，為剩下的經過做了補充說明。忠實情人羅密歐把要給父親的信，托僕人在他死後送過去，而這封信也證實了好心修士的供詞。信中，羅密歐說自己和茱麗葉結了婚，請求父母諒解；他也提到他向窮藥師買毒藥，打算去墓裡尋死，和茱麗葉躺在一起。

P. 88 　　這些細節之間完全沒有出入，修士就沒有了參與這場複雜凶殺案的嫌疑。他原是一番好意，卻因為方法太過詭譎造作，而導致了這些始料未及的結果。

　　親王轉身向柯孟兩位老爺，指責他們不該懷著殘暴又荒謬的仇恨，表示上帝因此給了他們的過錯這等懲罰，甚至藉由子女的一場戀愛來處罰他們這種人為的仇恨。

P. 89 　　這兩家世仇於是同意把宿怨都埋進孩子的墳墓裡，從此不再敵對。柯老爺請孟老爺把手給他，稱他為大哥，看似是承認了柯孟兩家年輕人的婚姻讓他們成了親家。他說，他為女兒所

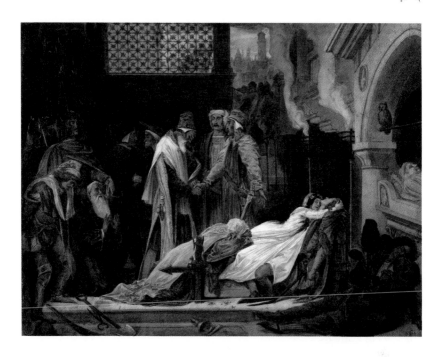

要求的所有贍養費就是孟老爺的手（以作為和好的象徵），但孟老爺說他要付更多的贍養費，為她鑄一尊純金雕像，只要維洛那城名聲不墜，忠貞茱麗葉的雕像就會是天下最華麗精緻的雕像。柯老爺接著表示，他也要鑄一尊羅密歐的雕像。

　　當事情已經無可挽回時，這兩個可憐的老家長才爭著對彼此示好。他們舊日的仇恨怨氣那麼深，只有經過子女可怕的死亡（是他們爭執不和之下的可憐犧牲品），才消除了這兩家貴族之間根深柢固的仇恨。

連環錯

P. 100　溪洛窟和以弗所兩國不合。以弗所制定一條屬法，明文規定溪洛窟的商人只要在以弗所市被發現，就得繳贖金一千馬克，否則一律處斬。

　　有人在以弗所街上發現溪洛窟的老商人葉吉，他被押去見公爵，看是要繳大筆罰金，還是接受死刑。

　　葉吉沒有錢付罰金，公爵在宣判他的死刑之前，要他說明自己的身世，以及為何明知溪洛窟商人踏進以弗所市會被處死，仍冒死前來。

P. 102　葉吉說他不怕死，因為他早痛不欲生了。要他講他那不幸的一生，才是最痛苦的事。以下，他開始說出自己的故事：

　　「我在溪洛窟出生，從小就學做買賣。我娶妻後，生活過得還算幸福。有一次，我要去掖披丹一趟，因為做生意的關係，我在那裡待了半年。後來知道自己還得停留更久，就請妻子也一道過來。她人一到，就生下兩個兒子。很奇怪，兩個兒子長得一模一樣，根本沒辦法分辨誰是誰。

我妻子生這對孿生兄弟時，在她下榻的客棧裡有另一個窮人家的婦女也生了兩個兒子。這對雙胞胎也和我兩個兒子一樣，彼此長得非常相像。因為他們的父母親太窮，所以我就買下他們，想說養大後可以侍奉我的兩個兒子。

P.104　　我的兒子長得很英俊，妻子深感驕傲。她日夜想著回家，我只得答應。我們在不祥的時刻上了船，因為我們從掖披丹出航還不到一里格的距離時，就刮起可怕的暴風雨。風雨愈來愈大，船員們眼看大船不保，為了逃命，他們就擠上小艇，把我們丟在船上，我們隨時都可能被狂風大浪給淹沒。

我妻子一直哭，那些不知道害怕的可愛孩子看到媽媽在哭，也跟著哭了起來。我自己並不怕死，但看到他們哭，我為他們感到惶恐，一心只想著如何可以保護他們的安全。我學航海人那套對抗暴風雨的方法，把小兒子綁在一根備用小船桅的一端，另一端則綁著孿生奴僕的弟弟。我教妻子如法炮製，把另外兩個孩子也綁在另一根船桅上。

P.107　　她看著兩個哥哥，我看著兩個弟弟。我們又各自把自己綁在綁著孩子的船桅上，要不是靠著這個方法，我們早就死了，因為船撞上了大礁石，都撞碎了。我們抓著細長的船桅，在水面上漂浮。我要照顧兩個孩子，無法顧及我的妻子，不久她就和其他兩個孩子與我分散了。他們還在我的視線範圍內時，被一艘（我認為是）哥林斯來的漁艇救了起來。

而後我便專心地和怒濤狂浪搏鬥，以保全我親愛的兒子和小奴僕。最後我們也被一艘船救了起來。那些水手認得我，很親切地招呼並幫助我們，把我們安全地送到溪洛窟的岸上。但從那個不幸的一刻起，我就再也沒有妻子和大兒子的下落了。

P. 108　　現在，我唯一在意的人就是我的么兒。他十八歲時開始打聽母親和哥哥的下落，時常央求我讓他帶著奴僕出去找他們。他的那個奴僕，就是那個也和哥哥失散了的小奴僕。最後我勉強答應了他，我是很渴望得到妻子和長子的消息，可是讓我的么兒去找他們，我也可能失去他和小奴僕啊。

　　如今，我兒子離開我已經有七年了。這五年來，我走遍世界，到處尋找他們。我到過希臘最遠的邊境，穿越亞洲，沿著海岸回來，在以弗所登陸，只要是有人跡的地方，我都不放過。但我這一生就要在今天落幕了，只要能夠確知我的妻子和兩個兒子都還活著，那我就死也瞑目了。」

P. 110　　不幸的葉吉說完了他的悲慘遭遇後，公爵很同情這個不幸的父親，他因為疼愛失散的兒子才落難。公爵說，他的職權地位不允許他擅改法律，要不是因為有違法令，他大可把他給放了。最後，公爵並沒有依照嚴格的法律規定將他立刻處斬，而是給他一天的時間去籌錢來付罰金。

　　對葉吉來說，這一天的寬限又有何用？他在以弗所人生地不熟，要找人借他一千馬克來付罰金，談何容易。沒有人可以搭救，何從釋放？他在獄卒的押解下，從公爵那裡退了庭。

　　葉吉以為他在以弗所沒有半個熟識，可是就在他遍尋么兒而性命堪虞時，他的么兒和長子卻恰巧就在以弗所城內。

P. 111　　葉吉的兩個兒子不僅容貌和身材完全一樣，連名字也都叫做安提弗，而另外那一對孿生奴僕，也都取名拙米歐。葉吉的么兒是來自溪洛窟的安提弗，老人家來以弗所，就是為了找他。好巧不巧的是，安提弗帶著奴僕拙米歐，和父親在同一天來到了以弗所。他也是溪洛窟商人，和父親的處境一樣危險。但幸虧他遇見了個

友人，通知他有個溪洛窟老商人落難的事情，勸他冒充成掖披丹商人，他也接受了友人的建議。聽到自己的同胞處境危急，他很難過，只是萬萬沒想到，這個老商人就是自己的父親。

P. 112　　葉吉的長子住在以弗所已經有二十年了（姑且稱他是「大安提弗」，以便和弟弟「小安提弗」做區別），而且還是個富人，有力能支付金錢，贖回父親的性命。只不過大安提弗對父親一無所知，他和母親被漁夫從海上救起來時，年紀還很小，只記得被救起來的樣子，對父母親都沒有印象了。把大安提弗、母親和小奴僕拙米歐救起來的漁夫，從母親身邊帶走了兩個小孩（這位不幸的婦人傷心極了），打算賣掉他們。

　　漁夫把大安提弗和大拙米歐賣給了知名的軍人梅納封公爵。他是以弗所公爵的叔父，他去以弗所探訪他的公爵姪兒時，隨身也帶了這兩個孩子。

P. 113 　　以弗所公爵很喜歡大安提弗，等大安提弗長大後，就讓他在自己的軍隊裡擔任軍官。大安提弗驍勇善戰，在沙場上建功，還救了提拔他的公爵一命。公爵於是就把以弗所一位富家姑娘雅卓安娜賜婚給他。在父親來到以弗所時，大安提弗已和雅卓安娜住在一起（他的奴僕大拙米歐也侍候著他）。

　　小安提弗和那個建議他冒充成掖披丹人的友人分開後，就遞給奴僕小拙米歐一些錢，要他先帶著錢到準備用餐的客棧去，表示自己要去鎮上蹓躂一下，看看當地的風土民情。

　　小拙米歐是個很得人緣的傢伙。小安提弗發悶發愁時，他會用奴僕那種古怪幽默和逗趣的俏皮話來自娛娛人。也因此，比起一般的主僕關係，小拙米歐對小安提弗講話的樣子就顯得比較隨便。

P. 115 　　小安提弗打發小拙米歐走了後，兀自站了半晌，尋思自己孤身一人到處尋找母親和哥哥，至今每個地方都打聽不出半點下落。他悲傷地自言自語：「我就像海洋中的一滴水，出去尋找自己的水滴同伴，結果在茫茫大海之中迷失了自己。我如此不幸，想找母親和哥哥，結果卻連自己也迷失了。」

　　就在他想著令人疲憊又毫無結果的尋人之旅時，（他以為）小拙米歐回來了。他納悶他怎麼這麼快就回來，便問他把錢擱在哪裡了。然而，現在和他說話的這個人並不是他自己的小拙米歐，而是攣生哥哥大拙米歐，和大安提弗住在一塊。這一對拙米歐和這一對安提弗，雙雙還是長得一模一樣，一如葉吉在他們嬰兒時期所見的一樣。因此也難怪安提弗會以為是自己的奴僕回來了，還問他怎麼這麼快就回來了。

P. 116 　　大拙米歐回答：「夫人要我請您回去吃飯。您再不回去的話，雞肉就要烤焦，肉串上的豬肉就要掉下來冷掉了。」

「現在不是開玩笑的時候。你把錢放在哪裡了？」小安提弗說。但大拙米歐仍自顧說著夫人要他來請安提弗回去吃飯，大安提弗問道：「什麼夫人？」

「老爺，當然是您的夫人了！」大拙米歐答道。

這個小安提弗還是個光棍，他對大拙米歐發脾氣說：「我平時跟你隨便閒扯慣了，結果就讓你這樣放肆地開我玩笑。我現在沒有心情開玩笑，錢呢？我們在這裡人生地不熟的，這麼一大筆錢你不好好保管，怎麼敢放心？」

大拙米歐以為那是他的主人，聽到他說他們人生地不熟，便認為是小安提弗在開玩笑，就開心地回答：「老爺，請您坐下來吃飯時再開玩笑吧。我只負責把您請回家，和夫人及夫人的妹妹一起吃飯。」

P. 118　　這下小安提弗再也忍不住，他揍了大拙米歐一頓。大拙米歐跑回家，告訴夫人說，老爺不肯回來吃飯，還說他根本沒有老婆。

聽到老公說他沒有老婆，大安提弗的太太雅卓安娜勃然大怒。她本來就是個醋罈子，老是說丈夫移情別戀。她開始鬧情緒，大罵丈夫，說著難聽的醋話。跟她住在一起的妹妹露希安娜，勸她不要無憑無據地瞎猜，但她聽不進去。

小安提弗回到客棧，看到小拙米歐仍帶著錢，安然無事地待在客棧裡。看到小拙米歐，他準備再罵他亂開玩笑時，雅卓安娜這時正好出現。她認定自己看到的人就是她丈夫，便開口大罵，說他看她的眼神有多怪異（這也難怪，他初次見到這位氣呼呼的婦人）；她說他結婚之前是多麼愛她，現在卻琵琶別抱。

P.120　「老公，是怎麼回事？你怎麼不再愛我了？」她說。

「這位夫人，您在問我嗎？」大吃一驚的小安提弗問道。

他跟她說，他不是她的丈夫，他來以弗所才待了兩個鐘頭，但她不理會，一定要他跟她回家不可。小安提弗脫不了身，只得跟她一道回他哥哥的家，和雅卓安娜、她妹妹一塊兒吃飯。她們一個叫他是丈夫，一個叫他是姐夫，弄得他莫名其妙，只好當自己在睡覺時娶了她，或是自己正在睡夢中。跟著一道前來的小拙米歐也一樣吃驚，因為嫁給他哥哥的那個廚娘，直喚他作丈夫。

就在小安提弗和嫂子吃飯時，真正的丈夫，也就是他的哥哥和大拙米歐想回家吃飯，但是僕人不肯放他們進門，因為夫人下令不讓任何人進來。他們一直敲門，當他們表示自己是安提弗和拙米歐時，女僕們都笑了出來。她們說安提弗正在和夫人吃飯，拙米歐也正在廚房

裡。他們都快把門敲爛了，還是進不了門。最後大安提弗氣呼呼地離開，聽到有個男人正在和他太太吃飯，他覺得太怪了。

P. 121　　小安提弗吃完飯後，那位夫人仍滿口稱他是丈夫，而且他還聽到連小拙米歐也被廚娘認作是丈夫。他百思不解，想找藉口，馬上逃出屋子。雖然他對妹妹露希安娜很有好感，但他並不喜歡愛吃醋的雅卓安娜，小拙米歐也很不滿意廚房裡的那位嬌妻，主僕兩人都巴不得盡快擺脫他們的新太太。

P. 122　　小安提弗一離開屋子，就碰上了金匠。金匠和雅卓安娜一樣，把他誤當成大安提弗。金匠叫了他一聲，遞給他一條金鍊子。小安提弗表示那不是他的東西，不肯收下。金匠只管回答那是依他的吩咐所打造的，說完就兀自離開，把金鍊子塞在他手裡。他想，自己在這裡遇到這些古怪的事情，一定是中了什麼法術，於是吩咐小拙米歐將行李打包上船，再也不想多留。

　　金匠把鍊子交出去之後，隨即因為一筆債務而被逮捕。金匠被官差逮捕時，已婚的大安提弗剛好打從旁邊經過。金匠以為已經把鍊子交給他，因此就跟他討金鍊子的錢。他剛給他的那條金鍊子的價錢，和讓他現在被補的債務差不多。

P. 124　　大安提弗說他沒有拿到鍊子，金匠堅稱自己幾分鐘前才交給他的。他們都認為自己沒有錯，兩人爭執了好一會兒。大安提弗不認為金匠給過他鍊子，但因為兩兄弟長得一模一樣，所以金匠咬定已經把鍊子交到他手裡。最後，官差因為金匠欠債未還，要把他押進牢裡，又因大安提弗不付金鍊子的價錢，金匠要求官差一併逮捕他。於是他們爭吵的結果，就是兩人雙雙被帶走押入牢裡。

在被押去牢裡的路上，大安提弗碰見了小拙米歐，他把弟弟的奴僕誤認為自己的奴僕，吩咐他去找妻子雅卓安娜，要她把那筆害他被捕的錢送過來。

主人才從剛剛吃飯的那個古怪房子裡倉皇逃了出來，小拙米歐不明白現在怎麼又要他回去。他本是來通知主人船要開了，可是他不敢答話。他看主人不像是可以開玩笑的樣子，就兀自離開。他咕噥著自己又得去雅卓安娜的家，說道：「到了那裡，陶紗貝又會說我是她丈夫了，可是我還是得去呀，僕人只得聽主人的吩咐。」

P. 125 雅卓安娜把錢交給小拙米歐，就在他要返回時，他碰到了小安提弗。小安提弗仍為一路上碰到的怪事感到納悶。哥哥在以弗所很有名氣，所以當他走在街上時，幾乎人人都向他打招呼，看起來就像是熟人舊識一樣。有人要還他錢，說是欠他的，有人邀請他到家裡坐坐，有人說承蒙他好意幫忙，要跟他道謝，這些人都誤把他當成是哥哥。還有一個裁縫師拿絲綢給他看，說是替他買下來的，一定得幫他量身，好做一些衣服。

小安提弗開始覺得自己闖進了巫覡之國。小拙米歐一點也沒有能讓主人解開困惑，還問官差本來要抓他去坐牢，他怎麼逃出來了，然後把雅卓安娜給他拿去付贖金的那袋錢交給他。

P. 127 小拙米歐說的什麼逮捕和坐牢的事，還有他從雅卓安娜那裡帶來的錢，完全把小安提弗給搞糊塗了。他說：「拙米歐這傢伙一定是精神錯亂了，我們在幻境中徘徊。」他感到混亂恐慌，大喊道：「求上帝把我們從這個鬼地方救出去吧！」

這時走來一個陌生人，這回是個婦女，也叫他安提弗。她說，他那天和她一起吃過飯，她跟他要一條金鍊子，他答應了要給她。

小安提弗再也按捺不住了，斥罵她是妖女，說他不曾答應過要送她鍊子，不曾和她吃過飯，甚至在這之前都不曾見過她這張臉。那位女子一口咬定兩人曾一起吃過飯，他也答應過要送她鍊子。小安提弗繼續否認，她於是又說，她已經給了他一枚昂貴的戒指了，如果他不給她金鍊子，她就要收回她的戒指。

P. 129　聽到這裡，小安提弗氣瘋了，直罵她是妖女、魔女，說自己從來就不認識她，也不知道她的什麼戒指，說完就跑開。聽到他這番話，又看到他憤怒的表情，女子愣在那裡。他們明明一起吃過飯，她也明明給過他戒指，所以他才答應要回送她金鍊子，這是再明白不過的事了。事實上，她和其他人一樣都搞錯了，誤把他當成他哥哥，做那些事的是

已婚的大安提弗，而不是眼前這位小安提弗。

　　已婚的大安提弗被擋在自己的家門口後（屋裡的人以為他已經在裡面了），便忿忿地離開。他的妻子最愛吃醋，他猜她一定是又吃了什麼飛醋。他想起她老愛亂冤枉他去找別的女人，為了報復她把他關在門外，他決定去找那位女子吃頓飯。那女子對他很客氣，被妻子這樣一番欺負之後，他就答應把原本打算送給妻子的金鍊子轉送給她。那條金鍊子後來被金匠誤交給他弟弟了。

P. 130　　女子很高興能有一條漂亮的金鍊子，所以也就回送已婚的大安提弗一枚戒指。當他說他根本不認識她、氣呼呼地走開時，她想他一定是發瘋了（她把他弟弟誤當成是他）。於是她當下決定去找雅卓安娜，說她丈夫瘋了。

　　就在她把這件事告訴雅卓安娜時，大安提弗由一名獄卒陪著回來（獄卒准他回家拿錢還債），而雅卓安娜派小拙米歐送去的那一袋錢，早已交給小安提弗了。

　　聽到丈夫責怪她把他關在門外，雅卓安娜相信女子說她丈夫發瘋的事情一定錯不了。她又想起那整頓飯下來，丈夫一直否認是她的丈夫，還說生平今天第一次來以弗所。她想他一定是瘋了，因此付錢打發獄卒走了之後，就吩咐僕人用繩索把丈夫綁起來，帶到暗室裡，差人去請大夫來醫他的失心瘋。大安提弗一直激動地喊冤叫屈，要怪只怪他們兄弟長得一模一樣。他愈是生氣，大家就愈是確信他發瘋。至於大拙米歐，他也和主人說同樣的話，所以也就一起被綁起來帶走。

P. 131　　雅卓安娜把丈夫關起來後不久，一名僕人跑來告訴她，安提弗和拙米歐一定是從守衛那裡逃脫了，因為他們現在正逍遙自在地在旁邊的大街上走著。

雅卓安娜一聽到消息，馬上帶了幾個人跑出去，要帶丈夫回來，而她妹妹也跟著一道出去。

當他們來到附近一家修道院的門口時，碰見了小安提弗和小拙米歐。因為這兩對雙胞胎長得實在太相像，她們又再度認錯人。

P. 132　　因長相酷似，造成這一片混亂，小安提弗為此納悶不已。金匠給他的鍊子就掛在他脖子上，金匠卻責怪他不該否認拿了鍊子而不肯付錢。小安提弗反駁，鍊子是今天上午金匠送給他的，而且他之後就沒再見過金匠了。

這時雅卓安娜走到他旁邊，說他是她發了瘋的丈夫，從守衛那裡逃了出來。她隨行帶來的人準備動手強抓小安提弗和小拙米歐時，他們溜進修道院，安提弗央求院長讓他們躲在修道院裡。

此時女修道院院長親自出來詢問吵鬧的緣由。她是個認真可敬的女士，有智慧判斷所看到的事情。她不想魯莽交出到修道院尋求庇護的男子，便細問夫人她丈夫發瘋的事情。她問：「妳丈夫為什麼突然發瘋？他是損失了海上的財產，還是死了個知己好友，讓他精神錯亂？」

P. 134　　雅卓安娜回答不是這些原因。

修道院院長說：「還是說他愛上了某家小姐，不再那麼愛妳，所以變成了這個樣子？」

雅卓安娜說，她早就懷疑他有外遇，才會常常不回家。

事實上，他並非另有他歡，而是妻子喜歡吃醋的個性逼得他有家難回（雅卓安娜激動的態度，讓院長猜出是這個原因）。為了得知真相，院長說：「那妳真得好好罵罵他才對。」

「有啊，我罵他了啊。」雅卓安娜回答。

院長表示：「唉，那可能是罵得不夠兇。」

雅卓安娜很樂意讓院長相信她已經充分和安提弗談過這件事情了。她說：「我們整天都在談這件事，床上談到這件事時，我就不讓他睡覺，餐桌上談到這件事時，我也不讓他吃飯。我們兩個單獨在一起時，我都只提這件事，有別人在時，我也常常暗示他這件事。我老是說，他要敢在外面拈花惹草，那是多麼不要臉啊。」

P. 135 從愛吃醋的雅卓安娜口中套出足夠的供詞之後，女院長說：「難怪妳的丈夫會發瘋。善妒的女人罵起來比瘋狗咬人還兇。看來是妳鬧得他不能睡覺，難怪他會頭昏腦脹。他吃肉時要配妳的責罵吃，吃飯吵吵鬧鬧會消化不良，所以他才會發燒發熱。妳說他在做娛樂消遣時，妳也會鬧得他玩不下去，既然社交和休閒的樂趣都被剝奪了，他當然會悶悶不樂、絕望不安了。這樣說來，就是因為妳愛亂吃醋，所以才把妳丈夫搞瘋。」

P. 137 露希安娜想替姊姊辯解，說姊姊指責丈夫時一向都很溫和，然後又對姊姊說：「別人這樣說妳，妳怎麼都不回話呢？」

但院長讓她看清自己的過錯，她只得說：「經她這麼一說，我自己都想罵自己了。」

雅卓安娜對自己的行為感到慚愧，不過仍堅持要院長把丈夫交還給她。院長不許外人進修道院，也不想把那個不幸的人交給善妒的妻子去照顧，就決定要用溫和的方法來處理。她走進修道院內，吩咐人把大門關好，不讓他們進來。

在這多事的一天裡，因為這些孿生兄弟彼此酷似，所以造成了這麼多的誤會。另外，老葉吉所得到的一天寬限，也眼見要結束了。現在太陽即將西沉，日落時如果還繳不出罰款，那就只有死路一條。

P. 139　葉吉接受執刑的地方就在修道院附近。院長剛走進院裡，葉吉就來到了這裡。公爵親臨現場，他表示，如果有人肯替葉吉出這筆錢，他可以當場赦免葉吉。

這時雅卓安娜攔住這個悲悽的隊伍，高喊要公爵主持公道，嚷著院長不肯把她發瘋的丈夫交還給她照顧。就在她說這話時，她真正的丈夫和僕人大拙米歐從家裡逃了出來，他們也來到公爵面前請求伸張正義，申訴妻子誣賴他發瘋，把他監禁起來，又說明他如何把自己鬆綁，從守衛的監守下逃出來。

看到丈夫，雅卓安娜大吃一驚，她以為他在修道院裡面。

P. 140　葉吉看到這個兒子，認定他就是那位離開他去找母親和哥哥的兒子，並且相信寶貝兒子一定會立刻為他付贖金。他用做父親的慈祥口氣跟他說話，心裡很高興，想著自己馬上就可以獲救。

P. 141　　然而讓葉吉驚愕不已的是，這個兒子說他根本不認識他。他當然會這樣說了，因為這個安提弗小時候在暴風雨中和父親失散後，就再也沒見過面了。可憐的老葉吉努力要兒子認出他來，他想，一定是自己太過焦急哀愁，變得怪模怪樣，所以兒子才會認不出他來，再不然就是兒子看到父親淪落至此，羞於承認。就在一陣混亂之中，女院長和另一對安提弗及拙米歐走了出來。看到兩個丈夫和兩個拙米歐就站在面前，雅卓安娜目瞪口呆。

　　這下子，這些莫名其妙、令眾人困惑不已的誤會立刻水落石出。看到這兩對安提弗和拙米歐雙雙長得一模一樣時，公爵立刻猜到這些離奇事件的原因了，因為他想到葉吉早上告訴過他的故事。他說，他們一定是葉吉的兩個兒子和孿生奴僕。

P. 142　　此時，還有一件意想不到的好事情，讓葉吉的一生獲得了圓滿。他早上被判死刑，還有那傷心訴說的往事，都在日落之前得到了快樂的結局——可敬的女院長表明身分，說她就是葉吉失散多年的妻子，是兩個安提弗慈愛的母親。

　　漁夫把大安提弗和大拙米歐從她身邊帶走後，她就進了修道院。由於她稟性聰敏，品德高尚，後來當上這家修道院的院長。當她好意收容一個不幸的陌生人時，也在無意中保護了自己的兒子。

　　這些失散已久的父母和孩子們興奮地互相祝賀，親熱地互相問候，一時之間，都忘了葉吉還被處了死刑。待大夥冷靜了些，大安提弗把贖金交給公爵，要贖回父親的性命。公爵很乾脆地赦免了葉吉，不肯把錢收下。

P. 143　　公爵陪同院長和她剛找回來的丈夫、孩子，一道走進修道院，聆聽這快樂的一家人漫談他們苦盡甘來的圓滿結局。我們

286

也不要遺漏了那對身分卑微的拙米歐的喜悅，他們相互祝賀問候，開心地恭維彼此的長相。在兄弟的身上看到自己長得這般俊俏（就像照鏡子一樣），他們好不歡喜。

經婆婆的一番諄諄教誨之後，雅卓安娜受益匪淺，從此不再疑神疑鬼或是對丈夫吃醋了。

小安提弗娶了嫂子的美麗妹妹露希安娜。善良的老葉吉和妻兒在以弗所住了許多年。雖然這些讓人困惑的事情是真相大白了，卻不能表示日後就不會再有誤會發生。彷彿是為了要讓他們記住曾發生過的混亂，偶爾還是會發生一些可笑的混淆，這個安提弗和這個拙米歐，被誤認成那個安提弗和那個拙米歐，於是上演了一場輕鬆詼諧的連環錯。

無事生非

P. 154 　　梅西納皇宮裡住了兩位姑娘，一位叫希柔，一位叫碧翠絲。希柔是梅西納總督李歐拿多的女兒，碧翠絲是他的姪女。

　　碧翠絲個性活潑，希柔天性較為嚴肅，碧翠絲就喜歡說些俏皮話來逗逗堂妹。不管是什麼事情，輕鬆自在的碧翠絲總能拿來消遣一番。

　　這兩位姑娘的故事是這樣開始的：軍隊裡幾個高階的年輕人，他們驍勇善戰，剛結束戰役返國，在路過梅西納時特地前來拜訪李歐拿多。

P. 156 　　他們當中有亞拉崗的親王唐沛左和身為弗羅倫斯貴族的友人克勞迪，與他們同來的還有機智而不拘小節的帕都亞貴族班狄克。

　　這些訪客以前就來過梅西納，好客的總督待他們如老友舊識，把自己的女兒和姪女介紹給他們。

　　班狄克一進屋裡，就熱絡地和李歐拿多和親王聊了起來。不喜歡被排除在談話之外的碧翠絲，打斷班狄克說：

「班狄克先生，我倒奇怪你怎麼還在講話，又沒有人理你。」

　　儘管班狄克和碧翠絲一樣輕率多話，但班狄克還是不滿她那種隨隨便便的問候方式。他想，這麼出言不遜的姑娘，想必不是很有教養。他還記得上次在梅西納時，碧翠絲就老愛拿他開玩笑。

P. 158　　喜歡開別人玩笑的人，反而不喜歡別人拿他來開玩笑，班狄克和碧翠絲就是這樣的人。這兩個機智風趣的人以前只要一見面，就會你來我往，唇槍舌戰一番，然後搞得不歡而散。

　　因此當班狄克的話說到一半，就被碧翠絲打斷，還說什麼沒有人在聽他說話時，他就故意假裝沒有注意到她在場，說道：「什麼！親愛的傲慢小姐，妳還活著啊？」

　　剎時他們又展開舌戰。碧翠絲說她要把他沙場上所殺的人都吃掉，儘管她知道班狄克在這次的戰役中表現英勇。她又注意到親王很喜歡聽班狄克說話，所以稱他是「親王的弄臣」，這個嘲諷比其他的挖苦話都更讓班狄克覺得刺耳。

P. 159　　她藉由說要吃光他所殺掉的人，來暗指他是懦夫，但他自視為勇者，這種話他才不在乎。然而，一個機智聰明的人就怕被說成是小丑，因為這種指責有時會太過接近事實。聽到碧翠絲說他是「親王的弄臣」，班狄克氣得牙癢癢。

在貴客的面前，個性謹慎的希柔默不作聲。克勞迪留意到她人長得愈來愈標緻，他注視著她婀娜多姿的身材（她本來就是個容易令人傾心的姑娘）。親王興致高昂地聽著班狄克和碧翠絲的有趣鬥嘴，他小聲地對李歐拿多說：「這個姑娘性情活潑開朗，給班狄克當妻子一定是絕配。」

P. 161 聽到這項提議，李歐拿多答道：「啊，殿下呀，殿下呀，他們要是結婚，兩個人不出一個星期就會吵瘋的！」

儘管李歐拿多認為兩人不配，可是親王並沒有放棄撮合這兩個智多星的念頭。

當克勞迪陪伴親王從王宮裡回來時，親王發現他們一路上不只談到撮合班狄克和碧翠絲這事，克勞迪還談到了希柔。聽他談希柔的樣子，親王猜到了他的心思。親王樂見事成，便對克勞迪說：「妳喜歡希柔？」

對於這個問題，克勞迪回答說：「啊，殿下，我上次在梅西納時，是用軍人的心態來看待她，我心裡頭雖然喜歡她，但沒有時間談戀愛。現在，天下清平和樂，毋須掛念戰事，所以就想到了男女之事。腦海裡希柔的倩影，讓我想起我在出征之前就有的情意。」

P. 162 聽到克勞迪表白對希柔的感情，親王很感動。他半刻也沒耽誤，就請求李歐拿多同意將克勞迪納為女婿。

李歐拿多贊成了這門親事，親王也沒費多大功夫，就說服溫柔的希柔親自接受高貴的克勞迪的求婚。克勞迪一表人材，功業有成，又有好心親王幫忙撮合，很快就說動李歐拿多盡早擇日幫兩人舉行婚禮。

再過幾天，克勞迪就可以迎娶他的美麗女郎，但他抱怨這期間的日子太無聊。的確，不管是什麼事情，大多數的小伙子在專心期待某件事情完成之際，總會有幾許的不耐煩。親王為了排遣克勞迪的時間，就提出一個有趣的樂子：想個妙計把班狄克和碧翠絲送作堆。

P. 163　　克勞迪興奮地參與了親王的這個突發奇想，李歐拿多也答應要一起通力合作，連希柔都說她願意盡棉薄之力，幫堂姊找到一個好丈夫。

親王想到的點子是，男士們去讓班狄克相信碧翠絲迷戀他，希柔則去讓碧翠絲相信班狄克愛上了她。

親王、李歐拿多和克勞迪率先行動。他們等待時機，在班狄克安靜坐在涼亭裡看書時，親王和幫手們就站在涼亭後面的樹叢裡。他們故意離班狄克很近，讓他不得不聽到他們的談話。一陣閒聊之後，親王說：「李歐拿多，你來。你那天是告訴我什麼啊，你說你的姪女碧翠絲愛上了班狄克先生？我萬萬也沒想到那位姑娘會愛上男人呀。」

P. 164　　「是啊，殿下，我也沒想到。」李歐拿多回答：「最妙的是她竟會喜歡上班狄克，她表面上看起來和他很不合。」

為了引證自己所說的話，克勞迪還說這是希柔告訴他的，說碧翠絲很迷戀班狄克，要是班狄克拒絕她，她一定會傷心而死。然而，李歐拿多和克勞迪都覺得他是不可能會愛她的，因為班狄克一向喜歡嘲弄美女，尤其是嘲弄碧翠絲。

親王一邊聽，一邊裝出一副很同情碧翠絲的樣子。他說：「要是有人告訴班狄克這件事就好了。」

「那有什麼用？班狄克會拿這事來消遣的，這只會讓可憐的姑娘更加難過罷了。」克勞迪說。

親王說：「班狄克要是敢這樣，應該要把他絞死。碧翠絲是個出色的甜姐兒，她做什麼事都很精明——除了愛上班狄克這件事例外。」

P. 166 之後，他就示意大夥繼續往前走，留班狄克在那裡思索所聽到的話。

班狄克偷聽得很起勁，當他聽到碧翠絲愛上他時，他喃喃自語道：「這有可能嗎？風是這樣吹的嗎？」

待他們一行人離開後，班狄克開始推論說：「這不像是惡作劇，他們一派正經，話又是從希柔那裡聽來的，而且還一副很同情那位姑娘的樣子。她愛上了我！那我好歹要回應她，我沒想過要結婚，我說我要打一輩子光棍，那是因為我不認為我在世會有結婚的一天。他們說那位姑娘德貌皆備，這也的確是。他們又說她凡事精明，只差愛上了我。唔，愛上我又不代表她蠢。哎呀，碧翠絲走來了，這位姑娘今天看來還真漂亮。我從她臉上瞧出

幾分對我的愛意了。」

此時碧翠絲走近他，用慣有的尖酸語氣說：「要我叫你進屋吃飯，我是很不心甘情願的。」

P. 168 班狄克沒想過自己會像現在這樣客氣地對她說話。他說：「美麗的碧翠絲，謝謝妳，辛苦了。」

碧翠絲又說了兩三句魯莽話，然後離開。在她失禮的話語背後，班狄克認為他看到了她隱藏的柔情。於是他大聲說道：「我要是不心疼她，那我就是個大爛人。我要是不愛她，那我就是猶太人。我要弄張她的畫像來。」

這位先生就這樣掉進他們所設下的圈套，現在輪到希柔來設計碧翠絲了。為此，她差來她的兩個侍女烏蘇拉和瑪格莉特。她對瑪格莉特說：「好瑪格莉特，妳趕去客廳找我堂姊碧翠絲，她現在正和親王及克勞迪說話。妳小聲地跟她說，我和烏蘇拉在果園裡散步，正聊她的事。妳叫她偷偷躲在那個舒適的涼亭裡。太陽把那裡的金銀花曬熟，涼亭卻不准太陽進來，像個忘恩負義的寵臣。」

P. 170 這個希柔要瑪格莉特誘使碧翠絲躲進去的涼亭，就是班狄克剛才在裡面偷聽到談話的涼亭。

「我保證一定馬上就讓她去。」瑪格莉特說。

希柔接著和烏蘇拉走進果園裡。她對烏蘇拉說：「烏蘇拉，現在一等碧翠絲來，我們就在這條小路上來回走，然後只聊班狄克的事。我會跟妳說班狄克對碧翠絲是如何地著迷，當我一提到他的名字時，妳就負責把他捧得好像他是天底下最棒的男人。我們現在就開始吧，妳看碧翠絲像隻貼地的田鳧，跑來偷聽我們的談話了。」

說罷兩人便開始。希柔好像回答烏蘇拉的什麼話似的，說道：「不，真的，烏蘇拉，她太瞧不起人了，她就像岩石上桀驁不馴的野鳥。」

P. 172 烏蘇拉說：「妳確定班狄克真的迷上碧翠絲？」

希柔回答：「親王和我的未婚夫克勞迪都是這麼說的，他們要我轉告碧翠絲，但是我勸他說，如果他們愛護班狄克，就不要讓碧翠絲知道這件事。」

「那當然。要是讓她知道了，那就不妙，她會冷嘲熱諷的。」烏蘇拉回答。

希柔說：「嗳，說真的，不管是如何聰明、高貴、年輕或是俊俏的男人，她都會把他說得一文不值。」

「是啊，是啊，這麼挑剔實在不好。」烏蘇拉說。

「是很不好，但誰敢說她呢？要是我跟她說，我會被她譏笑得半死。」希柔回答。

「哦，妳誤會妳堂姊了！她不會這麼沒有眼光，去拒絕一位像班狄克先生那樣難能可貴的紳士。」烏蘇拉說。

P.173　　「他聲名是很好。說真的，除了我親愛的克勞迪之外，他是義大利最棒的男人了。」希柔說。

接著，希柔暗示侍女換話題。烏蘇拉說：「小姐，那您什麼時候要出嫁呢？」

之後，希柔回答說自己明天就要嫁給克勞迪。她要烏蘇拉跟她一起去挑幾件新衣服，想跟她商量明天該穿什麼才好。

碧翠絲始終屏氣凝神地聽她們說話。待她們一走，她就叫說：「我的耳朵怎麼這麼燙？這會是真的嗎？永別了，輕蔑與嘲諷！再會了，少女的高傲！班狄克，愛下去吧！我會回敬你的，用你柔情的雙手，馴服我一顆狂野的心吧。」

P.175　　透過個性開朗的親王的趣味妙計，他們兩個人中了計，互相愛慕對方。看到老冤家變成新交摯友，能目睹兩人互相中意後再見面的情形，一定很有趣，但我們現在先說希柔的不幸遭遇吧。明天本來應該是她的大喜日子，結果卻為希柔和父親李歐拿多帶來了悲哀。

親王有個同父異母的弟弟，和他一道從沙場回到梅西納。這個弟弟（名叫做唐降）個性陰鬱，貪心無厭，心裡頭老在打著歪主意。

他痛恨他的親王兄長。因為克勞迪與親王的交情很好，所以連帶地他也討厭克勞迪。他決定要阻撓克勞迪和希柔的婚事，讓克勞迪和親王痛苦，讓自己一逞幸災樂禍的痛快。他知道親王和克勞迪一樣，心思都放在婚事上。為了達到他缺德的目的，他雇用一個叫包拉喬的人。這人的心眼和他一樣壞，為了煽動這人，他用重金收買。

P.176　　唐降知道包拉喬在追求希柔的侍女瑪格莉特，就要他讓瑪格莉特答應當天晚上在希柔睡著後，穿上希柔的衣服，然後在希柔閨房的窗口邊和他聊天，讓克勞迪誤以為她就是希柔，以完成這個缺德的陰謀。

之後，唐降去找親王和克勞迪，說希柔是個不知檢點的女人，三更半夜還在房間的窗口和男人聊天。

現在是婚禮前夕，他自告奮勇說今晚可以帶他們去看，讓他們親耳聽到希柔在窗邊和男人聊天。他們便跟著一道去，克勞迪說：「我今晚要是看到什麼讓我不該娶她的事，那麼明天，我就要在和她成婚的教堂裡當眾羞辱她。」

P. 177 親王也說：「既然我幫助你追到她，那我也會跟你一起羞辱她。」

當晚，唐降帶他們到希柔臥房的附近。他們看到包拉喬站在窗戶下面，瑪格莉特則從希柔的窗戶口往外看，他們還聽到她跟包拉喬說話。瑪格莉特穿的那套衣服，親王和克勞迪也都看過希柔穿過，因此兩人就認定那人就是希柔小姐。

克勞迪（自以為）發現這件事後，非常憤怒。他對清白的希柔的感情，瞬間變成了恨。他決定如自己所說過的一樣，明天要在教堂裡揭發她。親王表示贊成，對於這個放蕩的姑娘，他想沒有什麼懲罰會太過分，因為她在嫁給高貴的克勞迪的前一天晚上，還在窗邊和男人聊天。

P. 179 隔天，大家都相聚來慶祝婚禮。克勞迪和希柔站在牧師面前，而這位又被稱為修道士的牧師要開始主持婚禮時，克勞迪用最激動的話，宣布無辜希柔的罪狀。聽他說這些莫名其妙的話，希柔很震驚。她溫和地說：「我的未婚夫還好嗎？他怎麼這樣胡言亂語？」

李歐拿多很吃驚，他對親王說：「殿下，您怎麼不說話？」

「我該說什麼？我才感到羞愧呢，竟撮合好友和一個不自重的女人結婚。李歐拿多，我以人格擔保，我、我弟弟和傷心的克勞迪，都看到而且聽到了她昨天半夜在房間窗口和男人聊天。」親王說。

班狄克聽了很詫異，他說：「這看起來不像是在舉行婚禮嘛！」

P.180　「的確，哦，天啊！」傷心的希柔回答道。說完，這個不幸的姑娘昏厥過去，像是斷了氣一般。

親王和克勞迪不管希柔有沒有甦醒過來，也不理會他們帶給李歐拿多的痛苦，就逕自離開教堂。憤怒讓他們的心腸硬如鐵石。

班狄克留下來，幫助碧翠絲讓希柔醒過來。他說：「小姐還好吧？」

P.181　「我看是死了。」碧翠絲傷心地回答。她愛堂妹，也清楚堂妹的德性，壓根就不相信那些毀謗的話。

但那可憐的老父親就不是這樣了，他相信孩子做了丟臉的事。希柔像死屍一樣地躺在他面前，他希望她永遠都不要再睜開眼睛。聽著他的這般哀嘆，令人鼻酸。

但老修道士是個明眼人，洞悉人性。當這位姑娘聽到自己被指控時，他細心留意她的神情。他先是看到她臉上漲滿羞愧的紅暈，接著天使般的白淨驅走了羞紅，他在她的眼裡看到某種火光，顯示親王指責她不貞的話子

虛烏有。他對這個傷心的父親說：「躺在這裡的這位無辜的可愛姑娘，如果沒有受到天大的冤枉，那你就叫我笨蛋；不用再相信我的學問和見識，或是年歲、身分和職務！」

P. 182　這時希柔從昏迷狀態中甦醒過來。修道士對她說：「姑娘，他們指控妳和哪個男人聊天？」

希柔回答：「他們那些指控我的人才知道，我不知道。」說完她轉向李歐拿多說：「哦，父親，如果您能證明有哪個男人曾在不合宜的時候和我說話，或是我昨晚和什麼人說過話，那您就別再認我，只管恨我，把我折磨到死吧。」

修道士說：「親王和克勞迪一定是有某種離奇的誤會。」他建議李歐拿多宣告希柔已經去世，他們兩人離開希柔時，希柔昏死了過去，所以他們會信以為真。他勸李歐拿多穿上喪服，為她立碑，舉行完整的葬禮儀式。

「這會有什麼結果？」李歐拿多問：「這有什麼用呢？」

P. 184　修道士回答：「宣告她的死訊，毀謗會轉為憐憫。這樣有好處，但我要的好處還不只這個。克勞迪要是得知自己的話逼死了她，那他腦海裡會溫柔地浮現出她的倩影。要是他真心愛過，他就會為她服喪。就算他真的認為自己的指控有憑有據，他還是會後悔自己那樣地指控她。」

這時班狄克說道：「李歐拿多，就聽修道士的忠告吧。雖然你也知道我很喜歡親王和克勞迪，但我以人格擔保，我不會跟他們洩漏這個祕密。」

李歐拿多被勸說完之後答應了。他悲傷地說：「我太難過了，就連最小的細線都能把我牽走。」

好心的修道士把李歐拿多和希柔帶離開，好好安慰他們，留下碧翠絲和班狄克單獨兩人。朋友們設計他們兩個人，想看他們現在見面的有趣樣子，結果卻變了調。大家現在一片愁雲慘霧，根本沒有尋歡作樂的心情。

P. 185　班狄克首先開口說：「碧翠絲小姐，妳一直在哭嗎？」

「嗯，而且我還會再哭上一陣子。」碧翠絲說。

「是。我相信妳的好堂妹被人冤枉了。」班狄克說。

「啊！能替她伸冤的人，才是我的朋友！」碧翠絲說。

「有什麼方法可以成為這種朋友？在這個世界上，妳是我最愛的人，我這樣說會奇怪嗎？」班狄克說。

碧翠絲說：「我也可以說我最愛的人是你，這不是謊話，但你不要相信我。我什麼都不承認，也不否認，我只為我堂妹感到難過。」

「我用我這把劍發誓。妳愛我，我也正式宣告我愛妳！來，吩咐我為妳做些什麼事吧。」班狄克說。

P.187 「殺了克勞迪。」碧翠絲說。

「啊！那不可能啊。」班狄克回答。他愛克勞迪這個朋友，他相信他是被利用的。

「克勞迪這樣毀謗、蔑視、羞辱我的堂妹，不就是個流氓嗎？我要是個男人就好了！」碧翠絲說。

「妳聽我說，碧翠絲！」班狄克說。

但碧翠絲根本不聽他

為克勞迪所做的辯解。她仍催促班狄克為堂妹申冤報仇，她說：「什麼和男人在窗邊聊天，說得好像真的一樣！親愛的希柔！她被冤枉了，她被誣告了，她被毀了！哦，這個克勞迪，我要是男人就好了！要不然，有人願意為我當個男子漢也行！但是勇氣逐漸化成禮貌和恭維。我無法祈禱自己變成男人，我只能作女人家，然後傷心地死去。」

「等等，好碧翠絲。我舉手發誓我愛妳。」班狄克說。

P.188 「要是愛我，就用手做些別的事，不要用來發誓。」碧翠絲說。

「妳真的認為是克勞迪冤枉了希柔嗎？」班狄克問。

「是，這就像我有思想或靈魂一樣千真萬確。」碧翠絲回答。

「好，我決定去對他下戰書。離開妳之前，我要先親吻妳的手。我舉手發誓，一定要克勞迪給我一個的交代！請等我的消息，並且惦念著我。去安慰妳的堂妹吧。」班狄克說。

碧翠絲懇求班狄克，用憤慨的話激起他的俠義之心，使他不惜為希柔去和好友克勞迪決鬥。就在這時，李歐拿多也要親王和克勞迪拿劍和他決鬥，因為他們傷害了他的孩子，讓她傷心而亡。兩人看著這個悲傷的老人，說道：「別這樣，我們不要決鬥，老好人。」

P. 189　　這時班狄克出現。克勞迪傷害了希柔，班狄克要他拿劍決鬥。克勞迪和親王對著彼此說道：「這是碧翠絲唆使的。」

就在這時，傳來了有力的證據，天理還給了希柔清白，要不然克勞迪會接受班狄克的挑戰，進行一場命運未卜的決鬥。

親王和克勞迪談著班狄克的挑戰時，一位地方法官將包拉喬當作犯人押到了親王面前。原來，包拉喬和友人聊起唐降雇用他去幹的勾當時，被旁人給聽到了。

克勞迪聽著包拉喬對親王的全盤招供。包拉喬說和他在窗邊聊天的人其實是瑪格莉特，她穿著小姐的衣服，讓他們誤以為是希柔小姐。克勞迪和親王於是不再懷疑希柔的清白，就算仍有疑心，也因唐降的潛逃而釋疑了。事跡敗露後，唐降為了躲開震怒的兄長，就逃離出梅西納。

P. 190　　克勞迪知道自己冤枉了希柔，非常悲痛，自責自己無情的話逼死了她。心愛希柔的情影，頓時浮現在他的腦海裡，那是他最初愛上她時的樣子。親王問他，聽到事實時，他的心是否就像被燙過一樣。他回答，聽包拉喬說那些話時，他感覺自己好像在吞下毒藥。

悔恨不已的克勞迪懇求老李歐拿多原諒他帶給他孩子的傷害。他誤信對未婚妻的誣告，他允諾說，為了心愛的希柔，不管李歐拿多如何懲罰他，他都甘之如飴。

李歐拿多給他的懲罰，是隔天早上就娶希柔的一位表親為妻。他說對方現在是他的繼承人，長相酷似希柔。因為是自己親口允諾的，克勞迪表示願意和這位不相識的姑娘成親，就算對方是個黑人也沒關係。

但他內心萬分哀傷，他在李歐拿多為希柔所立的墓碑前，懊悔悲痛，哭了一整夜。

P. 192 到了早上，親王陪著克勞迪前往教堂。好心的修道士、李歐拿多和他的姪女都已經來到現場，準備慶祝第二場婚禮。李歐拿多把許配給克勞迪的新娘介紹給他，新娘子戴著面紗，克勞迪看不到她的臉孔。克勞迪對這位戴面紗的姑娘說：「神聖的修道士在前，請妳把手交給我。妳若是願意嫁給我，我就是妳的丈夫。」

「我在世的時候，曾做過你妻子。」這位不知名的姑娘說。她揭開面紗，原來她並非（如她所偽裝的）姪女，而是李歐拿多如假包換的女兒希柔小姐。

克勞迪驚喜不已，他一度以為她死了。他興奮萬分，不敢相信自己的眼睛。親王看到這一幕也同樣吃驚，他大喊道：「這不是希柔嗎？不是那個已經死去的希柔嗎？」

李歐拿多回答：「殿下，她在被誣陷的時候，的確是死了。」

P. 194　　修道士答應說，婚禮結束之後，他會跟他們解釋這件奇蹟。當他正要開始主持婚禮時，班狄克打斷他，說他也要在同時間和碧翠絲成婚。

　　對這個婚事，碧翠絲有些異議。班狄克質問她不是愛他嗎？他聽到希柔這樣說的。在一番有趣的解釋過後，他們這才知道自己被設計，相信了對方的情意。他們本來無意，一場戲弄人的玩笑竟讓他們弄假成真。

　　妙計誘騙他們互萌愛意，他們已經深深愛上對方，現在什麼也不能動搖他們的感情。既然班狄克求了婚，如今不管人們如何勸阻，也都沒有用。他開心地繼續這場玩笑。他對碧翠絲發誓說：他是因為可憐她才娶她，因為聽說她害相思病快死了。碧翠絲回嘴說：她答應嫁給他，是因為看在別人大力勸說的份上，想救他的小命，因為聽說他日形憔悴。

P. 195　　這兩個不拘小節的智多星就這樣和解。在克勞迪和希柔完婚後，他們也成親了。最後，把故事做個結尾吧。策動陰謀的唐隆逃亡後被捕，押回了梅西納。對這個陰鬱而不安分的人來說，計謀失敗後，看到梅西納宮廷內喜氣洋洋地舉行盛宴，就是一種最嚴厲的懲罰了。

暴風雨

P. 210 海上有這麼一座島，島上的居民只有一名叫做普洛斯的老人和他的女兒米蘭達。米蘭達是個貌美的年輕姑娘，稚齡之時便來到這座島上，除了父親，印象中沒再見過其他人。

他們住在洞窟石室裡，裡頭分成好幾個房間，其中一間做為普洛斯的書房，專為藏書之用。普洛斯大部分的書籍都跟法術有關，當時的讀書人特別著迷法術，普洛斯也發現法術很管用。他意外地漂流到這座島上時，島上被一名叫做辛蔻雷的女巫下了魔咒，在他來到島上不久前，辛蔻雷才死去。那時有一些不願為辛蔻雷幹壞事的善良精靈，被囚禁在大樹幹裡頭，普洛斯用法術把他們釋放出來，此後這些溫和的精靈就歸順了普洛斯。眾精靈的首領是艾瑞爾。

P. 211 小精靈艾瑞爾個性活潑，沒什麼壞心眼，只是愛捉弄醜怪物卡力班。他看不順眼卡力班，因為卡力班是舊仇辛蔻雷的兒子。

卡力班一開始是在林子裡被普洛斯撿到，他長得畸形醜陋，連大猩猩都比他人模人樣。普洛斯把他帶回洞窟，教他說話，本想好好待他，怎奈母親辛蔻雷的不良遺傳，讓他什麼正事或本事也學不會，所以只能把他當奴隸，派他撿撿木柴，幹幹粗活。而負責使喚他工作的人正是艾瑞爾。

P. 213 如果卡力班懶惰打混，艾瑞爾（除了普洛斯，誰也看不到他）就會偷偷捏他一把，甚至把他絆倒，讓他摔進泥坑裡。接著艾瑞爾會先變成一隻大猩猩，對他扮鬼臉，再變成一隻刺蝟，在他跟前翻滾，嚇得沒穿鞋的他深怕腳會被刺到。只要他沒有力行普洛斯吩咐的工作，艾瑞爾就會用這些整人把戲來折騰他。

再說有了這些神通廣大的精靈們來歸順，普洛斯也能呼風喚浪了。精靈遵從他的命令捲起狂風，使得海上的一艘大船，隨時可能被巨浪吞噬。普洛斯指著船對女兒說，船上載滿的是同他們父女一樣的人類。

305

P. 214　　　女兒說道：「哦，敬愛的爸爸啊！如果是您吹起了這場可怕的風暴，就請您可憐他們的不幸吧！您看，船都快要撞得粉碎了！他們好可憐啊，會死掉的呀！要是我有能力，我要讓大海和大地乾坤移位，這樣載滿寶貴生命的船就不會被吞沒了。」

　　　普洛斯說：「我的女兒米蘭達，妳不用怕，沒有人會受傷的。我已經下過命令，不可傷到船上任何一個人。我的寶貝孩子，妳可知我這麼做是為了妳啊！妳對自己或自己的身世都一無所知，對於我，你也只知道我是妳爸爸，住在這個簡陋的洞窟裡頭。妳還記得妳來到這個洞窟之前的事嗎？我想妳是不記得了，因為妳當時還不滿三歲。」

　　　「爸爸，我當然記得。」米蘭達答道。

　　　「記得什麼？」普洛斯問：「房子？人？孩子，跟我說妳記得什麼。」

P. 216　　　米蘭達說：「雖然過去感覺上像是一場夢，但那時是不是有四、五個女人服侍我呢？」

　　　普洛斯回答：「沒錯，而且還不只四、五個。妳記憶裡的印象如何？還記得妳是怎麼來到這裡的嗎？」

P. 217　　　「不記得了，爸爸。」米蘭達說：「我就只記得這些了。」

　　　普洛斯說：「米蘭達，在十二年前，我是米蘭的公爵，妳

是郡主，是我唯一的繼承人。我有個弟弟，叫做安東尼，我很
信任他。因為我喜歡閉關讀書，就常把政事交給妳叔叔，也就
是我那沒有道義的弟弟（他的確是沒有道義）。我醉心書堆，俗
務一概不管，把時間全用在修道上。我弟弟安東尼握有我的權
勢，竟然就真把自己當成公爵了。我給了他親民的機會，他的
壞心腸就起了壞心眼，想要奪取我的公爵的地位。不久強權敵
國那不勒斯王相助舉事，他便遂其所願了。」

P. 218　　米蘭達問：「他們當時有想要把我們殺掉嗎？」

　　　　父親回答：「孩子，他們不敢，因為我的子民很愛戴我。
安東尼要我們上一條船，行駛幾里格後，強迫我們換搭小船，
那一艘小船連根纜繩、風帆或船桅都沒有。他把我們丟下，以
為這樣我們就活不成了。殊不知宮裡一位很敬愛我的好心大臣
剛則婁，偷偷在船裡擺了水、食物和衣服，還放了一些我覺得
比公國都還珍貴的書呢。」

P. 219　　「爸爸啊！」米蘭達表示：「我那時候一定是您的拖油瓶！」

　　　　「不是的，寶貝。」普洛斯回答：「妳是護佑我的小天使，

妳的純真笑容支撐我渡過了難關。我們漂流到這個荒島時，船上的食物都還夠用。米蘭達，從那時候起，我最大的快樂就是教妳學東西了，而且妳也真的學到了許多。」

「敬愛的爸爸，我對您感激不盡。」米蘭達說：「但可以請您告訴我，您現在為什麼要製造這場狂風大浪呢？」

父親回答：「好吧，我告訴妳，因為這場狂風大浪會把我的死對頭那不勒斯王和我的狠心弟弟送到島上來。」

P. 220　話一說完，精靈艾瑞爾剛好出現，準備向主人報告暴風雨的情況，說明船上的人如何被處置。因此，普洛斯就用魔杖輕點女兒，讓她沉睡過去。米蘭達看不到精靈，但普洛斯可不想讓女兒以為他在和空氣講話呢（她應該會這麼想的吧）。

普洛斯問艾瑞爾：「勇敢的精靈，你任務辦得怎麼樣了？」

P. 221　艾瑞爾繪聲繪影地形容暴風雨和水手們驚恐的樣子。他說，那不勒斯王的兒子斐迪南最先躍入海裡，他父親見狀，以為兒子被海浪吞沒了。

「但實際上他是安然無恙的。」艾瑞爾說：「他現在正在島上的某一處抱膝而坐，為父王傷心欲絕，因為他也以為父親溺死了。事實上，這位王子不但毫髮無傷，他被海浪浸濕的皇袍看起來還更光鮮了呢。」

「真是我靈敏的艾瑞爾。」普洛斯說：「把他帶過來，我女兒要見見這位年輕王子。國王和我弟弟又在哪裡呢？」

艾瑞爾回答：「我讓他們忙著尋找斐迪南。他們親眼看到他落水，只能絕望地尋找他。船上沒有半個人失蹤，但每個人都以為自己是唯一的生還者。他們的船也安安穩穩地停靠在岸邊，只是他們看不到。」

P. 222　「艾瑞爾，」普洛斯說：「你的任務已經圓滿達成，不過還有其他差事。」

「還有其他差事？」艾瑞爾說：「主人，容我提醒您，您答應過要還我自由的。請您想想，我為您效勞，任勞任怨，從不說謊犯錯。」

「現在是怎麼了！」普洛斯說：「你忘了你是在什麼樣水深火熱的痛苦中被我救出來的嗎？你忘了年老善妒、彎腰駝背的邪惡女巫辛蔻雷了嗎？回答我，辛蔻雷是在哪裡出生的？」

「大人，她在阿爾及爾出生。」艾瑞爾回答。

「哦，是嗎？」普洛斯說：「看來你是忘了，我得把你的來歷再說一遍。邪惡的辛蔻雷女巫因為使用駭人聽聞的法術，被驅逐出阿爾及爾，水手們就把她流放到這個島上來。你是個心地善良的精靈，不肯服從惡毒的命令，所以就被她鎖在樹幹裡頭。我發現你的時候，你正苦苦哀號著。你要記得是我把你從這種苦難中救出來的。」

P. 224　「敬愛的主人，請您原諒我。」艾瑞爾為自己的忘恩負義感到羞愧，他說：「我會對您唯命是從的。」

普洛斯說：「你服從我，我就會還你自由。」說完就指示下一步命令。艾瑞爾離開後，前往剛剛丟下斐迪南的地方，而斐迪南仍憂心悄悄地坐在草地上。

　　「年輕的紳士啊！」艾瑞爾對著他說：「我現在要帶你走，好讓米蘭達小姐瞧瞧你的俏臉蛋。你得跟我走，走吧，先生，跟我走吧。」說完他接著唱：

> 令尊葬身五噚海底；
> 他骨骼化成珊瑚石；
> 他眼睛變成珍珠粒：
> 全身完好無一腐爛，
> 變幻瑰麗又甚奇妙。
> 海仙子時時敲喪鐘：
> 聽！我聞它叮噹響。

P. 226 　　父親的這個噩耗甚是古怪，王子從失神的狀態中驚醒過來。他心下詫異，跟著艾瑞爾的聲音走，直到碰見坐在大樹蔭影下的普洛斯和米蘭達。現在，米蘭達終於見到父親以外的第一個人類。

　　普洛斯問：「米蘭達，妳盯著那邊看是在看什麼呀？」

　　「爸爸！」米蘭達露出前所未有的訝異神情，說道：「想必他是個精靈吧。天呀！你看他東張西望的樣子！爸爸，真的，他真的是個美麗的動物。他是精靈吧？」

　　「女兒，他不是精靈。」父親回答：「他會吃會睡，跟我們一樣有知覺。他本來是那條船上的人，現在因為傷心而變得憔悴，要不然可稱得上是潘安再世。他和船上的其他人失散，正到處尋找他們。」

米蘭達還以為所有男人都長得跟她父親一樣，一臉嚴肅表情，蓄著灰鬍鬚。現在看到這位俊美的年輕王子，不禁心神舒暢。再說斐迪南，在這荒地看到如此花容月貌的女子，又聽到剛剛那些奇幻聲音，彷彿身處奇境仙鄉，以為自己到了仙島，逕自把米蘭達當成女神，稱她是女神地講起話來了。

P. 229　　米蘭達羞怯地表示自己不是女神，只是個普通的姑娘。

她正要自我介紹時，普洛斯插斷她的話。普洛斯樂見他們相互傾心，一眼就瞧出他們彼此一見鍾情（就像我們說的）。但為了考驗斐迪南的忠貞，他決定故意為難他們。他走向他們，嚴詞厲色地誣賴王子來島上是為了當間諜，想從他這個島主的手中把島奪走。

「你跟我來。」他說：「我要把你的脖子和兩腳綑在一塊，你只能喝海水，吃貝類動物、枯樹根和橡果殼。」

斐迪南回答：「休想，除非你打贏我，要不然我是不會乖乖就範的。」說完便拔出劍，誰知普洛斯魔杖一揮，他的雙腳就黏在地上，動也動不了了。

米蘭達抓住父親的手，說道：「爸爸，為何要這麼殘暴啊？可憐一下他吧！我可以擔保，這是我今生第二個見到的男人，看來是個正人君子。」

P. 231　父親回答：「女兒，你住口，你再多嘴我就罵妳！怎麼啦！想袒護騙徒嗎！妳只見過他和卡力班這兩個人，就以為他們的為人再好不過了。傻丫頭，我告訴妳，他比卡力班好很多。而大部分的男人又要比他好很多。」普洛斯這麼說，也是為考驗女兒的忠誠。

　未料女兒回答：「我對感情要求不多，就算有人比他更好，我也沒興趣。」

　「來吧，小伙子。」普洛斯對王子說：「你沒能耐抵抗我的。」

　「我的確是沒有。」斐迪南回答。他不知道自己被施了法，完全失去了反抗力量。他很詫異，自己竟莫名其妙、不由自主地跟著普洛斯走。他回頭望著米蘭達，直到看不見了為止。他跟著普洛斯走進洞窟，說道：「我好像在做夢，我的心被控制住了。不過，只要我在囚室裡能每天望著那名美麗女子一回，那麼，眼前這個人的威脅，或是我自己的無能為力，我都不當一回事了。」

P. 232　　普洛斯囚禁斐迪南沒多久，就把他帶出來，派給他困難的差事。普洛斯故意也讓女兒知道是什麼樣的差事後，就假裝走進書房，實則暗中觀察兩人。

　　普洛斯給斐迪南的差事是要他把一些笨重的木頭堆起來。這個國王的公子可不習慣這種粗活，米蘭達很快發現這個她鍾愛的人會累得出人命。

「哎呀！」她說：「你犯不著這麼賣力。我爸在看書，三個小時內都不會出來的，請你休息一下。」

「敬愛的小姐呀！」斐迪南說：「我不敢，我要完成工作之後才休息。」

米蘭達說：「你坐下休息，換我來搬木頭。」

但斐迪南不肯答應。這下米蘭達反而幫了倒忙，因為他們沒完沒了地聊起天來，結果木頭搬得還真得有夠慢。

P. 234　　普洛斯要斐迪南做粗活，是想試煉他的愛情。他並不如女兒所說的是在看書，而是躲在一旁偷聽他們講話。

　　斐迪南問她芳名，她告訴了他，還說父親不准她跟人報上自己的名字。

　　看到女兒這初次的違逆，普洛斯只是笑了笑，畢竟正是他用法術讓女兒立刻墜入情網的，所以不會生氣女兒為了愛情而違背他的命令。他也很得意地聽著斐迪南的一番傾訴，因為男方告訴女兒，說她是他這輩子最愛的女人。

米蘭達聽到斐迪南歌頌
她的美貌，說她絕色無雙，
便說道：「我腦海裡沒有任何
女人的影像，而且除了你這
位好友和我敬愛的父親，我
也沒見過其他男人。我不知
道島外的人長得如何，但你
要相信我，先生，在這世上
我只想和你作伴。除了你，
我再也想像不出還有什麼樣
的容貌會讓我動心。先生
啊，我說得太露骨了，把父
親的訓誡都給忘了。」

P. 236　　聽到這裡，普洛斯頷首笑了笑，彷彿是說：「事情進行得
正合我意啊，我女兒就要成為那不勒斯的皇后了。」

　　之後斐迪南又一番傾訴心曲，年輕王子講話果然就像個王
子，他跟純真的米蘭達說，他是那不勒斯的王位繼承人，所以
她會成為他的皇后。

　　「啊，先生！」她說：「我真傻，竟然為高興的事情掉眼
淚。我坦白、天真無邪地回答你，如果你要娶我，我就是你的
妻子了。」

　　也不等斐迪南對米蘭達表示感激，普洛斯驀地出現。

　　「別怕，孩子。」他說：「你們剛才所說的話我都聽到了，
我很贊成。斐迪南，如果我苛刻了你，那就讓我把女兒許配給
你來做為補償。我找些事情來刁難你，只是想考驗你的愛情，
現在你已經光榮通過考驗了。接受我的女兒吧，就當作是我送

給你的禮物，這是你真心真意的愛情所應該得的報償。你不要笑我是老王賣瓜，事實上，無論你怎麼讚美她，都不及她本人的好。」

P. 237　　接著，普洛斯說他得親自去處理一些事情，盼他們坐下來聊聊天，等他回來。看來，米蘭達一點也不想違抗這個命令了。

當普洛斯離開後就把精靈艾瑞爾給召來，艾瑞爾旋即出現，趕著說明自己如何處理普洛斯的弟弟和那不勒斯王。

艾瑞爾說他用異象幻聽，嚇得他們幾乎魂不附體。他們四處走，累了餓了時，他就忽然在他們面前變幻出餐宴美食。待他們伸手要吃時，他就變化成長著翅膀、貪得無厭的鳥身女妖出現，美食也頓時消失。

P. 239　　而最令他們驚恐的是，鳥身女妖跟他們說，他們狠心把普洛斯趕出公國，讓普洛斯和襁褓中的幼女葬身海底，而他們之所以會遇到今天這些恐怖的事情，就是因為幹了那些勾當。

那不勒斯王和不義兄弟安東尼聽了懊悔不已，後悔對普洛斯不仁不義。艾瑞爾告訴主人，他確信他們真心悔過，連他這個精靈也忍不住同情他們。

「艾瑞爾，那就把他們帶來吧。」普洛斯說：「你一個精靈都能感受到他們的痛楚了，和他們一樣同是人類的我，能不發點慈悲嗎？快把他們帶過來吧，可愛的艾瑞爾。」

艾瑞爾隨即在天上奏起奇妙樂聲，把國王、安東尼、老剛則婁等一行人，誘引到主人面前。這名剛則婁就是當年好心為普洛斯準備書籍和乾糧的那名剛則婁，那時狠心的弟弟把普洛斯扔在無一遮蔽物的小船上，要讓他命喪大海。

P. 240　　悲痛恐懼懾住眾人，他們沒認出來普洛斯。普洛斯走到好心的老剛則婁面前，稱他是救命恩人，這時弟弟和國王才認出原來他就是當年受害的普洛斯。

安東尼涕泗交流，誠心痛悔，請求哥哥原諒，國王也真誠地懊悔自己幫助了安東尼竊奪兄長的爵位。普洛斯原諒了他們。在他們保證歸還爵位時，普洛斯告訴那不勒斯王說：「我也有禮相贈。」普洛斯話一說完，就開了一扇門，讓國王看看正在和米蘭達下棋的兒子斐迪南。

再沒有比父子意外重逢更激動人心的事了，他們一度以為對方都在風暴雨中溺斃了。

「太奇妙了！」米蘭達說：「這些人類多高貴啊！他們住在那裡，那裡必然是個美麗世界呀！」

P. 242　　看到眼前這位絕色佳麗米蘭達，那不勒斯王和兒子一樣目瞪口呆。他問：「這位姑娘是誰啊？是讓我們離散又重聚的女神嗎？」

斐迪南回答：「爸爸，不是的。」看到父親跟自己一樣，初見她時就把她當作是女神，不禁莞爾一笑。他解釋：「她是個凡人，但上帝把她賜給了我。爸爸，我未經您同意就決定娶她，是因為我沒有想到您還活著。她是有名的米蘭公爵普洛斯的女兒，我早已久仰其大名，現在終於見到他的盧山真面目了。他讓我重獲

新生，可說是我的第二個父親，因為他把這位可愛的姑娘許配給了我。」

「那我就是她的父親了囉！」國王說：「不過這聽來好奇怪啊，我得請求我這個孩子原諒我。」

「別提了，」普洛斯說：「如今一切圓滿，就把舊日嫌隙都忘了。」

P. 243　　普洛斯抱住弟弟，重申自己已經原諒他了，還說充滿智慧、主宰萬物的神，之所以讓他被驅逐出可憐的米蘭公國，乃是為了爾後讓女兒得以繼承那不勒斯王位。正因這座荒島，他們兩人才相遇，王子才愛上米蘭達的。

普洛斯特意講這些好話來安慰弟弟，羞悔不已的安東尼泣不成聲。看到這種圓滿和解，好心的老剛則婆也感動得落淚，祈求蒼天保佑這對年輕情侶。

普洛斯這時告訴他們，他們的船很安全地停在岸邊，水手都在船上，明早，他就會和女兒同他們一道回家。

　　他說：「這會兒，到我的洞窟寒舍休息一下，吃點東西。我來說說我在荒島的生活，好當作今晚的餘興節目。」

P. 245　　他之後吩咐卡力班準備食物，收拾洞窟。看到這個醜八怪笨拙的動作和粗野的外形，眾人無不咋舌。普洛斯則表示，這是他唯一的僕人了。

　　離開荒島之前，普洛斯還給了艾瑞爾自由身，讓這個活潑的小精靈好不雀躍。雖然他一向對主人忠心耿耿，但總是渴望享受無拘無束的自由，可以像隻野鳥在綠林香果間、芬芳花叢上自由翱翔。

　　在還給他自由時，普洛斯說：「古靈精怪的艾瑞爾，儘管我會懷念你，但你仍應去享受自由。」

　　「謝謝您，敬愛的主人，」艾瑞爾說：「但請先讓我用順風護送您的船回家，然後您再向幫助過您的這個忠實精靈道別。主人，等我自由了，我會過得很快樂的！」

P. 246　　艾瑞爾接著歡唱了這首悅耳的歌曲：

　　　　蜜蜂吮蜜處我同吸吮；
　　　　野櫻草花瓣間我棲身：
　　　　貓頭鷹啼叫時我蹲伏。
　　　　乘著蝙蝠背脊我飛舞，
　　　　但且心神俱暢逐夏日。
　　　　從今以後我要樂陶陶，
　　　　枝頭花朵之下過生活。

　　最後，普洛斯把魔法書和魔杖深埋地底下，決心收山不再碰法術。他制勝敵人，和弟弟與那不勒斯王言歸於好，已經了無遺憾。現在只待返鄉，收復公國，參加女兒和王子斐迪南喜氣洋洋的婚禮。國王說，待他們一回那不勒斯，就舉行隆重婚禮。

　　在精靈艾瑞爾的平安護送下，他們一路旅程愉快，不久重回那不勒斯。

悅讀
莎士比亞
經典名劇故事

羅密歐與茱麗葉
連環錯
無事生非
暴風雨

作者 _ Charles and Mary Lamb
前言／導讀 _ 陳敬旻
譯者 _ Cosmos Language Workshop
編輯 _ 安卡斯
校對 _ 陳慧莉
封面設計 _ 林書玉
製程管理 _ 洪巧玲
發行人 _ 周均亮
出版者 _ 寂天文化事業股份有限公司
電話 _ +886-2-2365-9739
傳真 _ +886-2-2365-9835
網址 _ www.icosmos.com.tw
讀者服務 _ onlineservice@icosmos.com.tw
出版日期 _ 2018年11月 初版一刷（250101）
郵撥帳號 _ 1998620-0 寂天文化事業股份有限公司

國家圖書館出版品預行編目資料

悅讀莎士比亞經典名劇故事 / Charles and Mary
Lamb 著；Cosmos Language Workshop 譯；
—初版. —[臺北市] : 寂天文化, 2018.11 面；
公分. 中英對照

ISBN　978-986-318-743-1（25K平裝附光碟片）
　　　1. 英語　2. 讀本

805.18　　　　　　　　　　　　107017178